A RIO DAM NOVEL

YOU HAD ME AT RIO DAM

BOOK ONE

AINSLEY MCHUGH

Published By

PUBLISHERS

www.owlpublishers.com

360 S Market St, San Jose, CA 95113,
United States.

Printed in the United States of America

DEDICATIONS

For K.E.

Charlotte

Thank you for always believing in me, sharing your amazing stories, and for a sexy lead name. Thank you for always loving the name, Daniella.

George

You are my sunshine, my love, and my world. Always believe in yourself and remember that everything is possible.

A special thank you to
R.K., D.K., M.P., S.S., & E.V.

Table of Contents

CHAPTER 1 – THROUGH THE LENS

The morning sun rose slowly over Manhattan, soft and gold like a secret whispered across the skyline. From the rooftop of the SoHo loft, the city stretched endlessly — a mosaic of steel, brick, and stories. Heat shimmered faintly against the buildings, still struggling to free themselves from dawn's pale embrace. Car horns hummed far below, merging with the distant rush of traffic crossing the Williamsburg Bridge.

Daniella Russo adjusted the focus ring on her camera, narrowing her eye against the viewfinder. Click. The shutter captured a lone rooftop pigeon perched on the rusted fire escape opposite her. Another click — a taxi streaked down the street below, a yellow blur swallowed by morning haze.

She exhaled, savoring the familiar weight of the camera in her hands. Photography wasn't just her job — it was a sanctuary. The world could shout, demand, unravel... but behind the lens, she held control. She could frame only what mattered. She could silence chaos with a single shutter snap.

Her hair, dark and loosely curled, spilled over her shoulders as she leaned forward to catch another angle. A soft breeze lifted a stray strand, brushing her cheek like a teasing whisper. She tucked it behind her ear and lifted the camera again.

Today wasn't just another shoot. Today was him.

Wander-Line Travel had contacted her weeks ago for a marketing collaboration, but the man behind the email —

Russell Kane — had a presence that bled through every message. Professional, yes. Direct, definitely. But there had been something else, too. Something she felt even through a computer screen.

A warmth.

A confidence.

A pull.

She reminded herself not to overthink it. She was here to work — nothing more, nothing less. She adjusted a reflector panel, checking the light.

"Daniella Russo?" The voice floated up from behind her — deep, warm, smooth in a way that instantly curled inside her stomach.

She turned.

And there he was.

Russell Kane stood with one hand resting casually inside his jacket pocket, the other holding a sleek black folder. The rising sun painted a halo of light around him, revealing the sharp lines of his jaw, the faint shadow of stubble that made him look effortlessly rugged. His hazel eyes — somewhere between whiskey and green — studied her with a focus that made her breath hitch.

He was taller than she expected, broad shoulders tapering into a lean frame that hinted at strength more functional than decorative. His hair, dark brown and slightly tousled, caught the light like a brushstroke.

He smiled. Not a salesman's smile, but something warmer — something that reached his eyes.

"Hi," he said. "Russell. Wander-Line Travel."

Her fingers slipped slightly on the camera. "Right. Daniella. Daniella Russo." She stepped forward to shake his hand before instantly regretting how eager she sounded.

His grip was firm, steady. Confident. But it lingered a second longer than necessary — enough for a spark to catch between them.

"You're the travel agent-slash-marketing director?" she asked, trying to recover.

"Something like that." His grin deepened. "I help people get lost. On purpose."

A laugh escaped her before she could stop it. "Then I guess I'm here to help them remember where they went."

"Exactly." His eyes glinted with something playful — or curious.

Daniella cleared her throat and gestured to the rooftop setup. "We're shooting test frames for the campaign today. You wanted something that shows the real New York — the hidden corners, the overlooked beauty."

"You captured that even in your portfolio," Russell said. "Places most people walk past without noticing."

She felt warmth creep up her neck. Compliments on her work always struck deeper than the ones about her appearance.

He moved beside her, looking out across the city. The wind brushed his jacket open, revealing a slate-gray shirt that fit him like it remembered every line of his body.

"So where do we start?" he asked.

Daniella lifted the camera and gestured toward a line of rooftops in the distance. "The city has its own rhythm in the mornings. I want to catch that pulse. If you don't mind—"

She raised the camera, instinctively framing him in the shot. She expected him to pose, to adjust his stance. But he simply stood there, hands resting in his pockets, face turned slightly toward the light.

The sun kissed the edge of his cheekbone. His expression softened into something thoughtful, almost vulnerable. He wasn't modeling — he was simply being.

"Don't move," she whispered.

Click.

The shutter snapped.

In that instant — that fragile sliver of time — something

shifted. A breath caught. A pulse stuttered. A thread tightened between them, invisible but undeniable.

She lowered the camera slowly.

Russell blinked, breaking the moment. "So... good start?" he asked lightly.

She nodded, unable to trust her voice.

Their morning unfolded effortlessly—talk of hidden waterfalls in the Catskills, forgotten lighthouses along the Hudson, abandoned rail lines outside Bedford. He knew New York's secrets in ways no guidebook ever could.

But as he talked, Daniella noticed something else: He carried sadness beneath his smile.

A shadow tucked behind his easy charm. A story she didn't know yet — but wanted to.

Hours slipped by. The sun climbed higher. Eventually, Russell checked his watch.

"I should get going. I have a meeting this afternoon." His tone softened. "But... I'd love to show you some locations upstate next week. You'll want them for the campaign. They're unforgettable."

Her heart fluttered. "I'd like that."

He hesitated — just a breath — then offered her that warm, disarming smile again. "Good. I'll pick you up."

He turned to leave, but paused, looking back at her. "You're different from most photographers I've worked with."

"How so?" she asked.

"You don't just capture moments." His gaze dipped briefly to her lips before lifting back to her eyes. "You feel them."

The words sank into her chest, deeper than she expected.

And then he was gone, disappearing down the stairwell.

Daniella exhaled slowly, her fingers tingling against the camera still hanging from her neck. She replayed the moment — the light on his face, the sound of his voice, that last look he gave her.

Something had started today.

Something she wasn't ready for — but couldn't stop even if she tried.

She lifted her camera again, focusing on the empty space where he had stood.

Click.

The shutter closed on nothing but sunlight — and yet somehow, the frame still felt full.

CHAPTER 2 – THE PERFECT SHOT

The following week arrived with earlier sunsets and cooler breezes. Manhattan had slipped into that rare liminal window between seasons — the air still warm from summer, the shadows long like fall. Daniella packed her camera equipment carefully in her small SoHo studio, double-checking lenses, battery packs, and memory cards.

Today wasn't just another assignment. Today meant seeing Russell again.

She tried not to analyze the way her pulse fluttered as she zipped her backpack closed. She told herself it was excitement for the photoshoot, for the locations he had promised. But deep down, beneath layers she didn't fully understand yet, she knew it was more.

A soft knock sounded at her door.

When she opened it, Russell stood in the hallway. And once again, her breath caught.

He wore a simple black T-shirt and dark jeans, but somehow he looked like he had stepped out of a travel magazine. His hair was slightly damp — he must have showered right before coming — and the scent of cedar and clean soap drifted faintly toward her.

"You ready?" he asked, voice warm.

She nodded, trying not to stare too long. "Let me grab my

tripod."

He chuckled. "Take your time. We've got all day."

But there was something layered in his tone. Something that didn't sound like he was talking only about the shoot.

They walked out to his SUV — a dark gray vehicle with a few subtle scratches on the doors, the kind that came from years of driving on back roads. Russell tossed her backpack gently into the backseat and opened the passenger door for her.

"You don't have to play chauffeur," she teased.

"I'm old-fashioned," he replied. "And my mother taught me manners."

It was a small thing, but it made her smile. Inside the car, the faint scent of pine hung in the air, along with something else she couldn't place — something uniquely him.

As they pulled into traffic, he shot her a sideways glance. "Nervous?"

"Only about whether you're a good driver or not."

He laughed. "I'll try to impress you."

The drive north unfolded like an ever-changing tapestry. The city gradually softened, giving way to rolling hills, orchards, and winding two-lane roads flanked by fiery autumn leaves. Music played low on the stereo — a playlist of acoustic guitar, soulful voices, and songs that felt like late-night confessions.

"You picked this?" she asked.

He shrugged. "I like quiet music for long drives. Gives me space to think."

"What do you think about?"

His fingers tightened on the wheel. "A lot of things."

The way he said it tugged at something inside her.

They drove for nearly two hours before Russell finally slowed, turning onto a narrow dirt road framed by trees heavy with leaves that rustled in the wind. The air smelled of damp earth, pine, and something crisp and clean that the city had long forgotten.

"You said this was one of your favorite spots?" Daniella asked.

He nodded. "My fiancée and I used to come up here all the time."

The words hit harder than she expected.

Fiancée.

She kept her expression neutral, but she could feel a sharp tug in her chest. She shouldn't feel jealous — she barely knew him.

"She must love the outdoors," she said gently.

"She does." He paused. "Loved."

Daniella's head turned sharply. "Loved?"

He exhaled. "She's been… distant. Different. It's complicated."

She didn't push. She didn't need to. Something about the heaviness in his tone told her the story was twisted with more than simple heartbreak.

They reached a clearing overlooking the Hudson Valley. A glittering sheet of water stretched below, calm and luminous under the late afternoon sun.

"Rio Dam," Russell said quietly. "The town calls it the mirror of the valley."

Daniella stepped forward, breath catching as she took in the view. The dam stretched wide and stoic, its concrete spillway carved like a line between stillness and chaos. The water beyond it shimmered a soft silver-blue, broken only by the occasional ripple.

"It's… beautiful," she whispered.

"Wait until you see it at sunset," Russell said.

She lifted her camera, adjusting her settings as she scanned the treeline, the slope of the rocks, the curve of the dam. She inhaled slowly — savoring the calm. The quiet. The whisper of wind brushing past her ear like a welcome.

"You really love this place," she said without looking at him.

"I grew up not far from here," Russell replied. "My dad used to bring me fishing down by those rocks. Before he—" He stopped, swallowing hard.

"I'm sorry," she said softly.

He nodded. "It was a long time ago."

She didn't ask more. Trauma had its own silence, and she respected it.

"You know, this place isn't always quiet," he continued. "My friends and I used to dare each other to come here after dark." He paused, then added in a lower voice, "Someone vanished here once."

She turned sharply. "Vanished?"

He offered a small, almost crooked smile. "Just an old small-town rumor."

But Daniella saw something flicker across his face — doubt.

Or fear.

She was about to ask more when a sudden breeze swept in, catching her hair and sending her scarf fluttering like a ribbon. Russell stepped forward instinctively, his fingers brushing her cheek as he tucked a loose strand behind her ear.

Her pulse jumped.

He froze — the way a man freezes when he realizes he's crossed an invisible line. His breath caught. For a moment, neither of them moved.

A warm feeling settled in her stomach.

Then his phone buzzed.

He flinched, pulling his hand back quickly. "Sorry, I—" He stepped away, answering the call. "Ashling? Yeah. No, I'm here... I'll head home soon."

Ashling.

The name sliced neatly through the moment between them.

He hung up slowly, guilt tightening his jaw.

"We should get going," he said quietly.

"Of course."

They walked back to the SUV in silence. The tension between them pulsed — unspoken, electric, and dangerous.

The sun began its slow descent behind the valley, cloaking the dam in golden light. Daniella paused one last moment, lifting her camera.

Click.

The shutter captured the curve of the dam, the shimmering water, and a small silhouette far in the distance — someone standing near the treeline, watching them.

Daniella blinked.

When she looked again, the figure was gone.

CHAPTER 3 – BEHIND HER SMILE

The café sat on the corner of a quiet street overlooking the Hudson — a picturesque little place with flower boxes and mismatched tables, the kind people flocked to in the summer but forgot about the rest of the year. Daniella loved it instantly. It was quaint without trying too hard, warm without drowning in pretension.

What she didn't expect was to face the very woman who held a place in Russell's life she couldn't touch.

Ashling Moore.

The moment Daniella walked in, she spotted Russell at a corner booth. His shoulders looked tense but eased slightly when he saw her. She gave him a small smile and made her way toward him.

Before she reached the table, a woman slid gracefully into the booth opposite Russell.

Daniella froze.

Ashling.

She was stunning — a quiet, luminous kind of beautiful. Pale skin, sleek mahogany hair pulled into a low knot, green eyes that seemed too still to be entirely warm. She carried herself like someone who knew exactly how she was perceived and how to use it when necessary.

When Russell stood, greeting her with a gentle, almost cautious touch on her shoulder, Daniella felt something sharp twist inside her chest.

He hadn't expected Ashling to show up. That much was clear.

He hesitated only a second before introducing them.

"Daniella... this is Ashling."

Ashling extended her hand with a smile that shimmered just beneath the surface. "Hi. I'm Ashling. I've heard a little about you."

"Daniella Russo," Daniella replied, shaking her hand. Her voice remained steady, but inside her stomach tightened.

"Russell showed me your work," Ashling said, settling gracefully into her seat. "You capture people like you're reading their thoughts."

There was something in the way she said it — a lightness in tone, an edge in meaning.

"Thank you," Daniella replied.

Ashling stirred her coffee slowly with a silver spoon, eyes watching Daniella over the rim of her cup. "Just be careful," she added casually. "Some thoughts aren't meant to be read."

Silence stretched between them.

Russell cleared his throat. "Ashling stopped by unexpectedly," he explained quietly.

Daniella nodded, forcing a polite smile. "It's nice to meet you."

Ashling's lips curved slightly — not quite amusement, not quite sincerity. "Likewise."

But her gaze remained sharp. Too sharp.

Daniella focused on her portfolio binder beside her. She hadn't even gotten it open before Ashling leaned in closer to Russell.

"You didn't answer my call last night," Ashling murmured. Her voice was soft, but her words slid across the table like smoke.

Russell's jaw tightened. "I was busy."

"Busy?" she repeated, brow arching ever so slightly. "With her?"

Daniella blinked at the pointed shift in tone.

Russell's eyes widened with warning. "Ashling, don't—"

But Ashling leaned back, crossing her legs. Her composure didn't crack; it simply sharpened.

"I'm just making conversation," she said. "Isn't that allowed?"

Daniella tried to speak, to diffuse the tension, but Ashling's gaze caught her mid-breath. Something in Ashling's eyes pinned her in place — not malice, but calculation.

This woman was reading her. Measuring her. Evaluating her.

What for?

Daniella didn't know.

But she felt it.

Ashling turned back to her coffee, smiling again — this time perfectly. "You two make quite the creative team," she said. "Just be careful out there."

"Careful?" Daniella echoed.

Ashling's spoon paused mid-stir. "Yes. You never know what you'll find near the dam."

Daniella's heart gave a small, involuntary jump.

Russell swallowed hard. "Ashling, enough."

"Just making conversation," she repeated pleasantly.

But Daniella caught the look she gave Russell — a look that didn't belong to a fiancée on the verge of heartbreak. It belonged to someone hiding something. Someone planning something. Someone who knew far more than she let on.

When Ashling's phone buzzed, she reached for it and stood.

"I need to take this."

As she walked away, Daniella's gaze followed. Ashling stepped outside, her posture perfect, but her expression — just before she turned away — held a crack. A flicker of worry. Fear? Or guilt?

The door swung shut behind her.

Russell exhaled heavily. "I'm sorry," he said quietly. "She's been… distant lately. Different."

Daniella nodded. "Trouble?"

"Maybe." He rubbed his forehead. "She's not herself."

Daniella hesitated before asking, "Do you love her?"

He froze.

He didn't answer immediately — and that silence felt louder than any words.

"I did," he finally said. "Or I thought I did. Things changed."

Their eyes met across the small table. Something fragile and reckless shimmered between them.

Before she could read more into it, Ashling returned. Her expression smoothed into a calm mask as she sat beside Russell again, just a little too close.

"I have to go," she said, adjusting her coat. "Russell… we'll talk later."

Her gaze shifted briefly to Daniella, a look that seemed like a subtle warning.

Then she was gone, stepping into the cool air outside without looking back.

Russell dragged a hand down his face. "That went well," he muttered.

Daniella gave a soft, sympathetic laugh. "She seems… intense."

"She's unpredictable lately," he said. "It's like she's someone else."

Daniella waited, sensing he had more to say.

"She's been disappearing for hours," he continued quietly. "Not answering calls. Showing up randomly. And when she looks at me…" He shook his head. "It's like she's studying me."

Daniella's stomach tightened.

"Russell…" she said softly. "Do you think she's okay?"

He hesitated. "I don't know."

Outside, Ashling paused on the sidewalk. Through the window, Daniella caught one last glimpse of her.

Ashling stood completely still.

Her eyes fixed not on Russell.

Not on Daniella.

But on something across the street.

Daniella followed her line of sight.

A man stood at the end of the block — tall, wearing a dark jacket. His posture straight. Too straight. Too still. His gaze locked on Ashling.

The moment Ashling noticed Daniella looking, she forced a smile, lifted her hand in a small wave, and turned the corner.

Gone.

The man disappeared two seconds later.

Daniella's blood ran cold.

Something much larger was threading through Ashling's life. Something shadowed. Something dangerous.

And Daniella had the sinking feeling that whether she liked it or not...

She was being pulled right into the center of it.

CHAPTER 4 — AFTER HOURS

The rain came without mercy.

One moment, the Hudson Valley was muted under a gentle watercolor sky; the next, clouds cracked open and spilled a torrent of cold, relentless rain onto the world below. The air smelled like wet leaves, pine, and distant thunder.

"Run!" Russell called, grabbing Daniella's hand as the sky erupted.

They bolted across the gravel path, their laughter rising above the storm as they sprinted toward the old lakeside lodge — a rustic, cedar-sided building that had seen better days. Closed for renovations. Barely maintained. But dry.

Russell fumbled with the keys he'd borrowed earlier from management. "Come on, come on—" He jiggled the lock until the door gave way.

They stumbled inside, drenched, breathless, dripping onto the wooden floor.

The lodge smelled like cedar beams, old stone, and a hint of smoke from long-extinguished fireplaces. The lights flickered on overhead — warm, dim, and golden — casting soft glows across unfinished walls and empty chairs stacked in the corner.

Russell locked the door behind them just as thunder split the sky again.

Daniella, completely soaked, shoved wet hair out of her face. Drops clung to her eyelashes. Her pink sweater clung to her frame in ways she felt too exposed to acknowledge. She crossed her arms instinctively.

Russell turned — and froze.

His eyes dragged slowly across her silhouette, swallowing hard before he caught himself and looked away, swiping water from his brow.

"Guess we're stuck here awhile," he said lightly, voice tight with restraint.

She smirked. "You say that like it's a bad thing."

He huffed a soft laugh, running a hand through his dripping hair. "It's not."

A warm, charged silence settled between them. The kind that filled a room even louder than words.

"Here," he said suddenly, shrugging off his jacket. "You're freezing."

"I'm fine—"

"You're shivering."

Before she could argue, he stepped closer, draping the jacket over her shoulders. His fingers brushed the back of her neck — barely, but enough to send a shockwave right down her spine.

She swallowed hard.

"Thanks," she murmured, pulling it tighter around her.

Russell nodded, trying — and failing — to hide the way he watched her from the corner of his eye.

To break the tension, she took out her camera. "Let me get a few shots inside before the light dies."

He grinned. "You work even during storms?"

"Especially during storms. The lighting is unpredictable. Dramatic."

"Like you," he teased.

She nearly dropped the camera. "Excuse me?"

He shrugged and looked around the dim lodge. "You're dramatic. In a good way. You feel things intensely. I can tell."

She lifted her chin, refusing to let him read her that easily. "Maybe you just pay more attention than most people."

He stepped closer, slowly. Careful. Deliberate. "Maybe."

Her pulse quickened.

To distract herself, she snapped a few shots of the room: the large stone fireplace, the rain streaking down the large windows, the ghostly reflections of their silhouettes against the glass.

"Let me see," he said, stepping behind her.

He leaned in — too close. His chest brushed her back. His breath ghosted along her cheek. She lifted the camera slightly with trembling fingers.

"Here." Her voice barely worked.

The world shrank to the space between them. Between breaths. Between heartbeats.

He studied the screen over her shoulder, but she felt his attention on her far more than the photographs.

"You really are incredible," he murmured.

She turned her head before she could stop herself — and found his face already inches from hers. Her breath hitched.

"Russell..." she whispered.

Thunder cracked again, the lights dipped, and she startled — instinctively pressing against him. His arms came up reflexively, steadying her, holding her.

Their faces were so close she could feel the warmth of his breath.

"I've never met anyone like you," he said softly. His voice was deeper now, rawer. "You walk into a room and it's like... everything sharpens. Everything makes sense."

Her heart pounded in her chest so loudly she knew he must

have felt it.

"I shouldn't," he whispered, but he didn't move away.

"Neither should I," she admitted.

Their lips brushed — a feather-light ghost of a kiss.

Her grip tightened around the camera. His fingers curled lightly at her waist.

One breath.

Two.

Three.

But then Russell tensed suddenly and stepped back, breaking the spell with a sharp exhale.

"I can't," he said, running both hands through his hair. "Not yet."

Daniella blinked, breath still trembling out of her. "I know."

The rejection wasn't cruel — it was pained. Tormented. Stuck between longing and loyalty.

Russell raked a hand across the back of his neck, pacing a short line in front of her. "It's not that I don't—" He shook his head. "I do. God, I do. But with everything happening... Ashling... her disappearing, her acting strange... it's messy."

Daniella nodded. "I understand."

He stopped pacing and looked at her. Really looked. His expression cracked open — vulnerable, tired, scared.

"I don't want to hurt anyone," he whispered. "Least of all you."

Her breath softened. "You're not hurting me."

"But I could," he said. "You know that."

She pressed her lips together. "I'm not afraid of you."

The silence that followed was heavy and intimate. Not uncomfortable. Just full.

Outside, the rain intensified. Sheets of water slammed against the windows, lightning painting the sky white for brief, stunning flashes.

Inside, the world felt paused. Sacred.

"Come sit," Russell finally said, gesturing toward the small lounge area near the fireplace. "Let's talk. I feel like we've been speaking half-truths since we met."

She followed him to the oversized leather sofa. The cushions sank beneath her weight. He lit a lantern on the coffee table, the warm glow flickering across his face in a way that softened the lines of stress around his eyes.

They talked for nearly an hour.

About childhoods.

Dreams.

Failures.

Losses.

She told him how she hid behind her camera after losing too much, too young, how photography became her way of controlling the narrative when life had offered her none.

He told her about his mother's long illness, how helpless he'd felt watching the strongest woman he knew fade away. How Ashling had once been his anchor — steady, calm, supportive — until she wasn't.

He stared into the lantern's glow. "I feel like she's slipping through my fingers," he said quietly. "And I don't know if I should hold tighter or let go."

Daniella swallowed. "Have you asked her what's wrong?"

He hesitated. "I have. She always says she's fine. But something in her eyes…" He shook his head. "She looks like someone running from ghosts."

The words echoed in Daniella's mind. She remembered Ashling's face at the café — flawless, calm, sitting over something sharp and frightened.

Thunder rumbled again.

The lights flickered… then dimmed.

Daniella jumped, clutching his arm without thinking.

He covered her hand with his — warm, grounding. "It's okay. Storm's just sitting right over us."

She nodded, breathing in slowly. Her cheeks warmed at the closeness, but she didn't pull away. Neither did he.

For a moment, neither spoke.

The air was thick with unspoken things.

Desire.

Fear.

Curiosity.

Connection.

Russell brushed her knuckles with his thumb. A soft, absent gesture that made her pulse throb.

"Daniella..." he began.

She looked up.

Their eyes locked — fire, longing, restraint, and danger all colliding.

His voice dropped. "I don't think I've ever wanted someone as much as I want you right now."

Her heart stuttered.

"But I can't cross that line. Not while everything is so tangled."

She nodded, throat tight. "I know."

He pulled his hand back — reluctantly, painfully — like it physically hurt him to break the contact.

They sat in silence, letting the storm outside rage.

Minutes passed. Maybe hours. Time blurred in the warm lantern light and the sound of rain hammering the roof.

Eventually, the storm eased.

Russell stood. "We should head back before they close the roads."

She nodded.

As she packed up her equipment, he watched her — soft-eyed, conflicted, longing.

When they stepped outside, the air was cool, smelling of wet earth and pine. The rain had tapered to a fine mist. Faint moonlight shimmered across the surface of the lake like trembling silver.

Russell walked beside her toward the SUV.

Neither spoke.

Because words didn't fit into a moment like this.

Just as he opened her door, he paused.

"Daniella?"

She looked up.

He leaned in — not a kiss. Just a breath close enough to stir her hair.

"Whatever happens next...? I don't regret a single second with you."

Her breath caught. Her pulse thudded.

"Neither do I," she whispered.

He closed her door gently, circling to the driver's side.

Inside the SUV, the tension between them felt alive — like electricity strung tight, almost humming.

As they drove down the dirt road toward town, Daniella glanced once into the rearview mirror.

A figure stood near the trees.

Still.

Silent.

Watching.

She blinked. And it vanished.

Suddenly, the night didn't feel quite so peaceful anymore.

CHAPTER 5 – ASHLING'S SECRET

The rain at Rio Dam didn't fall so much as pounded.

It battered the concrete spillway in a relentless roar, turning the world into a curtain of silver. Water poured over the dam's edge in a thick, churning sheet, crashing into the reservoir below with a force that made the ground hum.

Ashling Moore stood beneath it all, tucked in the narrow, shadowed alcove under the spillway where the old service road ended. Here, the sound was deafening, the air damp and cold, the concrete sweating with years of moisture and moss.

She pulled her hood tighter around her face, breath fogging in the frigid air. Her fingers shook — not from the cold, but from the weight of the choice she was about to make.

A beam of headlights swung into view, diffused by the rain. A dark pickup rolled to a stop on the gravel, engine humming low. The driver's side door opened with a groan.

Bryan.

He stepped out into the rain, shoulders hunched against the downpour. His jacket was already soaked by the time he reached her, boots splashing through puddles. The resemblance between them was subtle rather than striking — the same set of the jaw, the same tilted green eyes, though Bryan's were warmer, less guarded.

"You shouldn't have come," he said, wiping water from his

brow. His voice was low, edged with worry.

Ashling swallowed hard. Her throat felt raw, like she'd been screaming even though she hadn't said a word since she left the house that morning.

"I didn't have a choice," she whispered.

The words nearly broke her.

Bryan glanced around—instinctively scanning the tree line, the shadows beyond the underpass. "You picked the worst night for this."

"I picked the only night they wouldn't expect me to move," she shot back, a fragile thread of impatience weaving into her voice. "Bad weather buys time."

"Bad weather hides bodies," he said flatly.

She flinched.

He sighed, softening. "Ash... what's going on?"

Her hands tightened inside her sleeves. "They found me again."

The words hung between them, heavy as the storm.

Bryan's jaw locked. "Who?"

She hesitated, eyes lifting to his. Rain ran in small rivers down the concrete behind him.

"The people I used to work for," she said at last.

He swore under his breath, the word lost beneath the roar of water. "I thought that was over. You told me you burned every bridge, refused every call—"

"I did," she snapped. "But they don't take no for an answer. You know that."

Bryan dragged a hand through his wet hair. "You told me you were out for good. That coming back here, settling down, getting engaged—that was your way out."

Ashling's laugh was short and humorless. "You think an engagement ring stops a program like that?"

"So it is them," he said. "Not just one handler. The whole thing."

She looked away, throat tight. The rain muffled the world, but it couldn't muffle her memory of that last meeting—an unmarked office, a familiar emblem tucked into the corner of a folder, the same clipped, practiced voices.

You owe us, Moore. Operations like this don't just dissolve because you found yourself a small-town fiancé and a white-picket life.

"I can't say it," she whispered finally. "Not here. Not out loud."

Bryan stepped closer. His eyes softened even as his voice hardened. "You're talking about the agency."

She pressed her lips together.

"CIA?" he pushed.

Her gaze flicked sharply to his. "Don't say it."

"The fuck else am I supposed to call them?" he demanded. "You disappear for eight months, show up with new scars and dead eyes, and don't tell your brother what you got dragged into—"

"I was trying to protect you," she hissed.

"And how's that going?" he shot back. "You meet some sweet travel agent, pretend to be normal, and now you're calling me in the middle of a storm under a dam like we're in a bad spy movie? Ash, what are we doing?"

Her shoulders sagged.

Rain drummed above them, an endless, punishing cadence.

"I got a message," she said quietly.

He stilled. "From who?"

"They don't sign their names." She slipped a hand into her pocket and pulled out a small, battered phone. Not her usual one. A burner. "Coordinates. Time. Two words: reactivation approved."

Bryan swore again, softer this time.

"I thought they'd moved on," Ashling continued. "I thought I'd done enough. Enough time, enough damage, enough lying. But they want me back in. There's something happening here, Bry. At Rio."

His gaze swept the water, the dam, the vast valley beyond. "Here? In this town?"

"Some kind of field operation. They called it RIO last time I... overheard something. Recruitment, asset placement, and local cover. It was already spinning before I left."

"So that's why you came back here," he said slowly. "Not just for nostalgia."

Ashling swallowed. "This place was always more than childhood for me. It became... convenient. Familiar terrain. Easy for them to plug me back in."

"And Russell?" he asked.

The name hit her like a stone dropped into still water.

She didn't answer at first.

"Is he convenient too?" Bryan pressed. "Or is he just collateral in all of this?"

Her jaw trembled. "He wasn't supposed to be anything."

"But?"

"But he is," she said hoarsely.

Bryan's shoulders sank. The protective big-brother side warred visibly with the soldier who understood tactics, leverage, and collateral damage.

"They're watching him," she admitted. "Watching who he knows, who he talks to, where he goes. I thought… if I stayed close, if I controlled the variables, I could keep him out of the worst of it."

"And how's that going?" Bryan demanded. "You're spiraling, he's suspicious, and now there's this photographer in his life who looks at him like he's the first breath after drowning."

Ashling flinched.

"I met her," she said quietly.

"Daniella?"

"Yes." She wrapped her arms around herself. "She's… dangerous."

Bryan frowned. "The photographer? She looks like she reads romance novels and drinks overpriced coffee."

"She sees people," Ashling said sharply. "Too clearly. Russell doesn't realize how exposed he is with someone like that around. She notices things."

Bryan gave a humorless smile. "It's not her job to notice things. That's yours."

Ashling's eyes narrowed. "I'm not joking, Bry."

"I know you're not," he said. "That's what scares me."

She leaned back against the slick concrete, eyes closing for a moment.

"When I met Russell," she began, voice softening, "he was... uncomplicated. Kind. He loved itineraries and flight deals and making people believe in vacations. I was a cover identity with a backstory that checked out. A job, a family, a past scrubbed just enough. He fell for the version of me they created."

"Ash—"

"I let him," she continued. "Because for the first time in years, I wanted to believe I could be her. That I could be..." She hesitated on the word. "Normal."

Bryan's expression softened. "You're more than what they made you."

Her laugh was brittle. "Tell that to the files they keep on me."

He shifted closer. "So what do they want now?"

"Information," she said. "Access. A foothold. Something about this town, this dam, the people moving through it. It's not just random tourists and locals anymore. They think something's brewing. An exchange, a contact, a leak—maybe all three."

"And you're supposed to what? Cozy back up to Russell, smile pretty, and feed them his entire life?"

Her stomach turned. "Something like that."

Bryan studied her face. "Do you think he's involved? Even unknowingly?"

She shook her head instantly. "No. He's good. He's... annoyingly good. Too honest for this world."

"But?" he pressed gently.

"But I don't trust the pattern," she whispered. "He's central in too many ways. The travel agency, the local partnerships, the bookings, the seasonal retreats. People move through him. And people are what they care about."

Bryan rubbed his jaw. "So what are you going to do?"

"I need to disappear," she said, voice flat with finality.

The words seemed to echo off the concrete.

He stared at her. "You're serious."

"I don't have a choice," she replied. "If I stay, they pull me back in and use him against me. If I cooperate, they own him. If I refuse, they erase me. You. Everyone who knows too much."

He swallowed. "You think they'd go that far?"

"You know they would."

Silence pressed in, thick and suffocating.

Rain hammered the dam. Water thundered below.

"I got a call last night," she added quietly. "Unknown number. Same cadence as my old handler; they don't change their rhythm. He said one thing before the line cut out: 'You had your fun, Ashling. Time to come home.'"

Bryan's hands curled into fists. "They're not your home."

"They're my owners," she said bitterly. "Or they think they are."

He stepped closer, gripping her shoulders. "Listen to me. You are not theirs. You have a choice."

"That's the problem," she said, voice breaking. "Every choice I have puts someone in danger."

He looked into her eyes, searching for the sister he knew before years of covert operations, lies, and missions that never existed on paper.

"Then let me help you," he said. "This time, you don't disappear alone."

"Bry—"

"I mean it," he cut in. "Tell me what you need. Tell me what's coming. Tell me who to watch for."

She hesitated, glancing toward the distant road.

Headlights occasionally flashed far above the dam —
unrelated cars, harmless travelers.

For now, "Don't believe what they tell you," she said finally,
voice low. "If anything happens... if I go missing, if they say I
ran, relapsed, cheated, stole, snapped—don't believe it."

His throat worked. "Ash—"

"You will hear things," she insisted. "Stories. Reports. Neat
little narratives wrapped up with official stamps. None of it will
be true. Or all of it will be half true." Her eyes glistened.
"Promise me you won't let them write my ending."

Bryan's voice roughened. "I promise."

She exhaled shakily. "Don't trust Russell completely, either."

His eyebrows shot up. "Excuse me?"

"I don't know if he's connected," she said quickly. "But
they've got lines into everything. Travel routes, agencies,
contracting, town councils. If he's on a list somewhere, even
by accident, they'll tap him. I can't risk that. So keep your
distance. Take nothing at face value. Not from him. Not from
them. Not even from me if it looks too clean."

He stared at her for a long moment.

"You really think this is that big?" he asked.

She smiled sadly. "You haven't read my file."

He huffed out a humorless breath. "I shouldn't have to."

The wind shifted, blowing mist into their faces.

In the distance, a low rumble that wasn't thunder rolled faintly through the valley—maybe a truck on a service road, maybe something else. Instinct prickled up Ashling's spine.

"They'll be watching soon, if they're not already," she said.

"Then we move now," Bryan replied. "I'll get you somewhere safe. Off-grid. I've got contacts—"

"You have friends," she corrected. "People with mortgages and kids and camp schedules. I'm not dragging them into this."

"You dragged me into it the second you said 'reactivation,'" he shot back. "That's not a word I can unhear."

Her eyes softened. "You don't have to fix this."

"You're my sister," he said simply. "I do."

For a moment, she looked younger — like the girl who used to swing her legs off the dock, daring him to jump in first. The girl who laughed too loud, ran too fast, believed too much.

That girl was buried deep, but not gone.

"Okay," she said finally. "There's one thing you can do."

"Name it."

"If I disappear," she said quietly, "make sure they don't bury the truth with me. Don't let them spin this town into another cautionary tale. Watch the dam. Watch the people around it. There's more going on here than missing women and accidents."

His eyes narrowed. "You mean the rumors? The disappearances?"

"They're not rumors," she said.

A chill skated down his spine.

"Ashling—"

She stepped past him, out from under the alcove. Rain instantly soaked her hood, her jacket, her jeans. She tilted her head up, letting the cold hit her face like a slap.

"I have to go," she said.

He followed her out into the rain. "Where?"

"Ahead of them," she replied. "Before they decide where I go next."

Lightning split the sky, briefly turning the entire dam pure white.

In that flash, Bryan saw something in her eyes — not fear. Not exactly.

Resolve.

Resignation.

A tiny, flickering hope.

He grabbed her wrist. "Ash, if you vanish, you know what this will do to Russell."

Her composure cracked, just for a second. "I know."

"You care about him," he said quietly. Not a question.

She let out a shaky breath. "More than I meant to."

"Then tell him," Bryan urged. "Tell him before you go."

"I can't," she whispered. "The less he knows, the safer he is. If he starts looking for me, they'll notice. They'll use him. They always use the ones who care."

She gently pulled her wrist free.

He let her go.

A truck horn sounded somewhere far above them on the main road.

"They're going to paint you as the unstable one," Bryan said. "You know that, right? They'll say you walked away. Cheated. Used him. Broke under pressure."

Her mouth twisted. "They've called me worse."

"Ash..."

She turned back one last time.

"If anything happens," she said, "don't believe what they tell you." Her voice dropped, hushed and fierce. "Especially not Russell."

"You think he could be involved?" he asked.

"I think he's more important to them than he realizes," she answered. "And I don't know which is more dangerous — him knowing, or him staying innocent."

Bryan stared at her, rain sliding down his face like tears he refused to shed.

"I'll help you disappear," he said at last. "But if it comes down to you or them..."

He couldn't finish the sentence.

She gave him a small, sad smile. "I've never expected to win, Bry. I just don't want to lose everyone else in the process."

She stepped backward, into the curtain of rain, then turned and headed toward the narrow trail that wound through the trees.

He watched until her form blurred into shadow.

Lightning flashed again, briefly outlining her silhouette near the service road before she vanished completely.

The storm swallowed her.

Bryan stood alone under the spillway, the roar of the dam shaking his bones.

Above him, water poured endlessly over the concrete edge.

Below, in the valley, a quiet town went about its business—unaware that somewhere in the rain, a woman was trying to outrun the people who had once owned her...

...and that the very place they all called home was the center of a game much bigger than any of them.

CHAPTER 6 – EXPOSURE

Three days passed without a word from Ashling.

Not a call.

Not a message.

Not a sighting in town.

Nothing.

For a woman whose presence always seemed to press into a room—even when she wasn't speaking—her absence felt like a vacuum. A silent wound carved into everything Russell touched.

And Daniella saw it happening.

She saw the exhaustion in his face, the dark circles beneath his eyes, the way he looked over his shoulder as if he expected someone to materialize out of shadows.

But she also felt something else building between them. Something they both kept pretending wasn't real.

It scared her.

It thrilled her.

It was becoming impossible to ignore.

Daniella stood in her studio, surrounded by the soft hum of drying prints and the faint scent of developer chemicals.

Sunlight slanted through the narrow windows, dust motes swirling lazily in its path. Her workspace was a controlled chaos of pinned photos, notebooks, sketches, and camera gear.

Today she was working through the second roll from Rio Dam — the one she hadn't fully examined yet.

She clipped one print to the drying line.

Then another.

And another.

All ordinary landscape shots.

Trees. Rocks. Water.

Until one wasn't.

She paused.

Something in the far corner of the frame snagged her attention — a dark shape near the treeline. A silhouette. Human.

She pulled the photo down, holding it closer to the light.

A woman.

Long hair. Slim build. Wearing a pale jacket.

Her breath hitched.

Ashling.

Daniella's fingers tightened around the photo. She examined the next frame.

There she was again.

Different angle.

Different distance.

Same jacket.

Same posture — head turned toward the camera, as if she knew she was being captured. As if she wanted to be.

Her chest tightened. A faint prickle crawled up the back of her neck.

She grabbed her phone.

You need to come see something, she texted Russell.

He replied almost instantly.

On my way.

He arrived twenty minutes later, knocking twice before letting himself in. He looked strained—hair messy, stubble thicker than usual, shoulders tense. His eyes scanned the studio until they found her.

"What's going on?" he asked.

She didn't answer. Instead, she pressed the photo into his hands.

He stared.

His breath caught.

"When was this taken?" he whispered, voice rough.

"Two days before she vanished," Daniella replied softly.

Russell swallowed hard, eyes darting between the photo and Daniella. "This… this can't be…"

"She was there that day," Daniella said. "At the dam. Watching us."

He looked at her sharply. "She never told me."

Daniella hesitated. "Russell… do you think she knew something was coming?"

He shook his head, jaw clenching. "I don't know what to think."

But Daniella did.

Ashling had been leaving clues.

Messages.

Breadcrumbs.

Someone like her didn't get photographed by accident.

And she certainly didn't stare directly into a camera unless she meant to.

Daniella watched as Russell dropped heavily onto her studio stool, running a hand over his face.

"I've called her parents," he said quietly. "Her friends. Bryan. No one's seen her. No one knows anything."

"Bryan?" Daniella asked.

"Her brother," Russell said, staring blankly at the photo. "He said she'd been acting strange. Withdrawn. He thought she was hiding something."

"Was she?" Daniella pressed gently.

He hesitated.

"Yes," he whispered. "But I didn't want to see it."

Daniella sat beside him, their knees brushing accidentally. He didn't pull away this time.

For a long moment, they sat there in silence. The air between them thick with things unsaid.

Finally, Russell exhaled shakily. "Can I see the rest?"

She nodded and handed him the stack of photos.

As he sifted through them, each shot revealing Ashling in different corners of the scenery, something darkened in his expression.

"This wasn't random," he muttered. "She was following us."

Daniella's pulse quickened. "Why?"

Before he could answer, her phone vibrated.

She glanced down.

Unknown number.

Her stomach turned.

The message contained a single line:

Stop.

Daniella's throat went dry. She showed Russell.

His face hardened. "We're not stopping."

Her phone buzzed again.

A second message.

She didn't want you involved.

Russell snatched the phone. "Who is this?"

A reply came immediately.

Ask the detective.

A chill ran down Daniella's spine.

"How would they know we're here?" Russell whispered.

Daniella thought of the figure she'd seen at the lodge.

The man across the street on the day of the café.

The silhouette in the photos.

"Someone's watching us," she murmured.

Russell's jaw tightened. "Then we go to the precinct."

"Russell—"

"We have to," he insisted. "Someone knows more. And Bowman's been on this from the beginning."

There was something in his voice — a blend of desperation and determination — that made her nod.

She grabbed her camera bag. He grabbed the photos.

Together, they headed toward the door.

But before they left the studio, Daniella paused.

"Russell?"

He turned.

Her voice was soft, barely controlled. "We're going to find her."

His eyes softened. The distance between them disappeared in two steps.

He cupped her face gently, forehead brushing hers. "I

know."

Their breath mingled. Warm. Fragile. Close enough to kiss.

Too close.

He stepped back first. "Let's go."

They stepped into the hallway.

Neither of them saw the shadow move at the bottom of the stairs.

Or the faint red blink of a tiny recording light.

The precinct was buzzing with tension when they arrived.

Phones rang. Officers moved briskly through the hall. A storm of activity churned around them — but none of it seemed directed.

Detective Bowman came from his office, expression tense. "Kane. Russo. Thought I might see you today."

He led them into a small interview room. The metal table gleamed under bright fluorescents.

"Tell me everything," he said.

Russell started from the beginning. Daniella added details when necessary. She slid the photos across the table.

Bowman examined each one carefully, his jaw tightening.

"When did you take these?" he asked.

"Last week," Daniella replied.

"She was there the whole time," Bowman murmured, tapping a finger on the edge of the last photo. "Not hiding. Not running. Watching."

"Do you think she was in danger?" Russell asked.

Bowman hesitated.

"Yes," he said. "But not from who the town thinks."

He tapped the photos again. "This doesn't look like a woman fleeing a cheating scandal or a nervous breakdown. It looks like a trained operative scanning her surroundings."

Daniella exchanged a startled glance with Russell. "Operative?"

Bowman's eyes darkened. "There are things about Ashling Moore I wasn't sure I should share yet. But after seeing these…" He pushed his chair back and stood. "I need to make a few calls."

He stepped out of the room.

The door clicked shut.

Russell sank into his seat, hands trembling.

"Are you okay?" Daniella whispered.

"No," he said honestly. "I feel like every day I wake up and learn a new thing about her. Things that don't make sense. Things I never imagined."

He lifted his eyes — and met hers.

"You're the only thing that feels real," he whispered.

Daniella's breath caught.

He leaned forward.

She did too.

Just as their lips were a breath apart—

The door burst open.

Bowman rushed in, eyes blazing.

"We have a problem."

They jumped apart, hearts pounding.

Bowman slapped a printout onto the table.

A grainy surveillance still.

Of Daniella.

And Russell.

Inside her studio.

Taken from outside the window.

"Someone's been tracking both of you," Bowman said.

Daniella's stomach dropped. "Who?"

Bowman's jaw flexed. "Whoever Ashling was running from."

Russell stood. "Bowman—you need to find her before something happens."

Bowman nodded. "I'm trying. But with this kind of operation?" He tapped the photo. "We're not dealing with amateurs."

He looked between them.

"You two need to be careful," he said. "Someone is watching every move you make."

And then he added, softer, almost reluctantly—

"And I'm not convinced Ashling Moore disappeared by accident."

On the drive back to the city, tension sat between them like a living, breathing thing. Rain streaked the windshield, flashing under streetlights like silver ribbons.

Daniella finally spoke. "Russell... when you look at those photos, what do you feel?"

He tightened his grip on the wheel.

"I feel like I never knew her at all," he said quietly. "And I don't know which version of her was the truth."

"Do you regret being with her?" Daniella asked softly.

He hesitated.

"I regret trusting someone who was lying to me," he said. "But I don't regret loving her. I only regret that she didn't love me enough to be honest."

Daniella's heart squeezed.

"And now," he said, voice raw, "I don't know if I'm grieving the woman I thought she was… or the fact that she lied to me from the beginning."

Daniella reached across the console, gently intertwining her fingers with his.

He didn't pull away.

He squeezed back.

Slow.

Certain.

Desperate.

Outside, lightning streaked the sky.

Inside the car, something fragile tightened between them — a quiet promise neither could name yet.

That night, when Daniella finally returned to her apartment, she set her camera bag on the floor and collapsed onto her couch.

The storm raged outside.

She stared at the photographs strewn across her table.

Ashling's silhouette.

Her face half-turned. Her posture still.

Watching. Waiting. Warning.

A shiver crawled up Daniella's spine. She picked up the last image. In the far background, at the edge of the frame— barely visible—stood another figure.

Not Ashling. Someone else.

Someone taller.

Broader.

Wearing a dark jacket.

Watching her.

Daniella's pulse thundered in her ears.

She grabbed her phone with shaking hands.

Russell answered instantly.

"Daniella?"

Her voice trembled.

"There was someone else at the dam."

Silence.

"Someone watching me."

Another silence.

Then, quietly— "I'm coming over."

And somewhere in the dark, on a quiet rooftop across the street, a man with a camera lens lowered his equipment. He made a note on a small pad.

Subject aware. Escalation imminent.

He snapped the notebook shut.

And waited.

CHAPTER 7 – THE DISAPPEARANCE

The Hudson Valley didn't wake up slowly. It jolted awake.

By dawn, the news had spread through town like wildfire, flickering from porch to porch, whispered in grocery aisles, carried across café counters, and murmured outside the church as early risers stepped into the cool morning breeze.

Ashling Moore was missing.

Her silver sedan had been found abandoned near the Rio Dam just before sunrise. Door unlocked. Keys in the ignition. Her favorite scarf — the soft cream one she always wore in autumn — caught on the guardrail like a ghost clinging to the morning wind.

Daniella heard it first from Russell.

He called her at 6:12 a.m.

She had barely slept after the discovery in her photos, the figure in the background, the shadow that seemed to move every time she blinked.

Her phone buzzed on the pillow beside her.

She snatched it up, heart pounding.

"Russell?"

His voice cracked. "She's gone."

Those words — raw, broken — were enough to make

Daniella sit upright instantly.

"What do you mean gone?"

"They found her car," he said tightly. "But not her. She—" His voice faltered. "She didn't just leave. Something happened."

Daniella pressed her hand over her mouth. The dread she'd been feeling hardened into something sharp.

"I'm coming," she said. "Where are you?"

"By the dam." His voice wavered. "Please... just come."

She grabbed jeans, a sweater, and slipped on boots without tying them perfectly. Her fingers shook as she locked her door. The storm had passed, leaving the morning cold, crisp, and eerily silent.

She drove with the window cracked, the smell of wet earth and pine filtering in, mixing with the thudding of her pulse.

When she arrived, multiple patrol cars blocked the pull-off near Rio Dam. Detectives clustered near the guardrail where Ashling's scarf hung, fluttering weakly. Yellow crime scene tape snapped in the breeze.

And there, standing alone near the railing, was Russell.

He looked hollow like someone had carved out the center of him and left only the shell.

Daniella walked toward him slowly. "Russell..."

He turned.

His eyes were red-rimmed, exhausted, tortured.

"She wouldn't leave her car," he said hoarsely. "She wouldn't leave her keys. She wouldn't…" He swallowed hard. "She hates the water. She wouldn't walk near the edge."

Daniella stepped closer. "Russell—"

"I should've done something," he whispered. "I should've seen how scared she was."

"Russell—"

"I should've asked her more," he said. "Should've paid attention. Should've—"

"Russell," Daniella whispered, gripping his arms.

He finally looked at her.

For a moment, the world stilled — only wind, water, and the two of them suspended in fear.

"You can't blame yourself," she said.

His voice was a rasp. "Then who do I blame?"

Before she could answer, Detective Bowman approached, his expression determined and grim.

"Kane," he said calmly. "I need your statement."

Russell didn't move.

Bowman looked at Daniella. His eyes softened. "You too."

They followed him toward the patrol car, where a folding table was set up with paperwork, evidence bags, and a laptop. Officers moved around them with practiced efficiency.

Bowman handed them each a clipboard. "Tell me everything. From the moment you last saw her to the second you realized something was wrong."

Daniella's stomach knotted. She and Russell exchanged a glance, then slowly began writing.

Behind them, the calm but forceful voice of an officer giving commands carried through the air. "Search along the west bank. Keep a twenty-foot spread. Check for footprints along the mudline."

The gravity of the scene surged around them.

An abandoned car.

A missing woman.

The dam's roar echoing through the valley.

This wasn't a misunderstanding. This was a disappearance.

And Daniella couldn't shake the memory of the silhouette

in her photographs.

Ashling, looking directly into the lens. As if she knew someone would search for the truth in those images.

A cold breeze swept across the dam. Daniella pulled her sweater tighter.

Beside her, Russell trembled subtly.

Bowman noticed. "Kane," he said gently, "take a break. Go get some air."

But Russell shook his head. "No. I'm fine."

He wasn't.

Not even close.

As the search expanded, townspeople gathered along the ridge above the dam, whispering.

"She hasn't been right."

"I saw her last week — she looked… haunted."

"Do you think she ran?"

"Or do you think someone—"

Daniella tuned them out.

Her attention was locked on the dam's edge.

A small flash of color caught her eye several feet down —

something lodged against the rocks near the spillway.

She moved closer, careful not to step past the tape.

A red fabric triangle.

Not a scarf.

A tag.

From a jacket. Her heart began to thrum.

"Bowman."

The detective turned toward her.

"What is it?"

She pointed. "There. Something red."

Bowman motioned to two officers. "Gear up. Check it."

Within minutes, they donned harnesses and descended the rocky incline.

One officer shouted up after a moment. "It's clothing!"

Bowman's jaw tightened.

Russell stood rigid. Frozen.

Minutes later, the officers climbed back up, holding a shredded red tag in a clear evidence bag.

"Looks like part of a jacket," the officer said. "Caught in the rocks. Could've been torn."

Russell's breath hitched. "She had a jacket like that," he whispered.

Daniella slipped her hand into his, squeezing gently. He squeezed back.

But her mind was racing.

Ashling had been there. Watching. Following. Leaving clues in her photographs. Leaving something else behind now.

But why?

Before she could form an answer, Bowman returned to them, eyes thoughtful.

"We're treating this as a missing persons case with suspicious circumstances," he said.

Daniella frowned. "Suspicious?"

Bowman nodded. "The abandoned car. The torn clothing. The position of the scarf. And—" His gaze flicked to Daniella. "The presence in your photographs."

Russell stiffened. "You think she was in danger?"

"I think someone knew where she'd be," Bowman replied. "Maybe more than one person."

Daniella's pulse raced.

"Bowman..." she said slowly. "Ashling wasn't alone the day we were at the dam."

Bowman's eyes sharpened. "The figure in the background?"

"No." She swallowed. "Another figure. In the last frame."

She pulled the photo from her pocket, handing it over.

Bowman studied it carefully. "This angle... the distance..." His brow furrowed. "This person has training. You don't stalk someone this professionally without experience."

Russell exhaled shakily. "Training? What kind of training?"

Bowman looked up, voice low. "Military. Intelligence. Law enforcement." He paused. "Or all three."

A shiver went down Daniella's spine.

Russell stared at the dam. "What the hell was she involved in?"

Bowman didn't answer.

By late afternoon, the formal search paused due to worsening weather and fading light.

Russell and Daniella stood near her car. The wind had grown sharper, slicing through damp clothes and chilled skin.

"You should go home," she said quietly.

He shook his head. "I can't."

"You haven't eaten."

"I'm not hungry."

"You need sleep."

"I can't sleep."

She stepped closer. "Russell... you can't torture yourself."

His eyes burned into hers. "What if she needs me? What if she left a clue? What if she's waiting?"

Daniella placed a hand on his chest — gently, feeling the erratic thump beneath.

"You're not alone," she whispered. "You have me."

He closed his eyes, inhaling deeply as if absorbing the strength she offered. His hand rose, fingers curling lightly around her wrist.

"I don't deserve you," he murmured.

"You deserve someone who cares about you," she whispered. "Let me be that person."

His eyes opened slowly.

For a moment — a fragile, trembling moment — he leaned in as if gravity itself was pulling him toward her.

She held her breath.

But at the last second, he pulled away, stepping back sharply, pained expression twisting his features.

"I can't," he whispered. "Not with her missing. Not with this happening."

Daniella nodded, pushing down the ache rising in her chest. "I understand."

She didn't push. She didn't withdraw. She simply stood there — steady, patient, painfully present.

Russell raked a hand through his hair. "Just... don't leave. Okay? I can't do this alone."

"You're not alone," she repeated softly.

He exhaled, something fragile in him softening. "Can I stay at your place tonight? Just to talk? I don't want to be alone with my thoughts."

"Of course," she said.

"Thank you."

As they headed to her car, neither noticed the figure leaning against a distant tree trunk.

Watching motionless.

A camera lens glinted faintly under the fading sun.

A small red light blinked.

Recorded.

Filed.

Sent.

The watcher scribbled in a notebook.

Subject R emotionally compromised. Subject D engaged. Operation momentum increasing.

The notebook snapped shut.

The figure melted back into the trees like a ghost.

And Daniella and Russell, unaware of the eyes tracking them from every angle, drove away into the dimming evening — toward a night that would bring answers neither of them was ready to face.

CHAPTER 8 – DETECTIVE MIKE BOWMAN

Detective Mike Bowman didn't intimidate easily.

He was built like the kind of man who had spent his twenties at the NYPD learning how to read the worst of humanity and his thirties figuring out how to live with the knowledge. Broad shoulders, thick forearms, a stiff gait from an old injury, and eyes that registered everything with startling clarity.

He had the face of a tired boxer and the brain of a chess master.

And he was standing at the edge of Rio Dam with a frown carved so deep it bordered on worry.

He didn't worry.

Ever.

Which made today different.

Very different.

The wind swept across the dam, sharp and biting, carrying the metallic scent of wet concrete and the restless churn of water. Officers combed the banks with drones and thermal scanners. A K9 unit searched the tree line. Flashing lights cast blue and red reflections across the reservoir's surface.

But Bowman wasn't looking at the water. He was studying Russell Kane.

The man stood rigid, hands shoved into his pockets, gaze locked on Ashling's abandoned car. His expression was a battleground — guilt, fear, grief, and confusion all circling like vultures.

Bowman approached him slowly.

"Kane," he said with a nod.

Russell didn't look up. "I already gave my statement."

"You did." Bowman tapped a pen against his notebook. "And now I need more."

Russell's jaw tightened. "I told you everything."

"You told me everything you know," Bowman corrected, eyes narrowing. "There's a difference."

Russell finally looked at him, frustration flickering. "I'm not hiding anything."

"That's what they all say."

Bowman's voice wasn't cruel — just firm, matter-of-fact. He had zero interest in coddling people or in making them feel comfortable. Comfort was a luxury the truth often didn't allow.

Daniella approached hesitantly, her presence soft against the hardness of the investigation. She held a thermos of hot coffee for Russell. He accepted it with trembling hands.

Bowman noticed.

He noticed everything.

"You two were together when these photos were taken," Bowman said, holding up the evidence bag containing Daniella's prints. "Explain it."

"We were shooting for his company," Daniella answered.

Bowman nodded. "Right. Wander-Line Travel. You two drove up together?"

"Yes," Daniella said.

"Stopped along the way?"

"Just for coffee," Russell replied.

"What about after the dam?"

Daniella exchanged a glance with Russell. "We... got caught in a storm and waited it out at a lodge."

Bowman paused, pen freezing mid-scratch.

"A lodge," he repeated. "Which lodge?"

"The one off Route 5," Russell said. "It's under renovation."

Bowman's eyes narrowed slightly. "You went inside a closed lodge?"

"I have a key for client retreats," Russell said. "It wasn't breaking and entering."

Bowman grunted. "You always bring photographers there?"

Russell stiffened. "We weren't doing anything wrong."

Bowman smirked. "Never said you were."

He jotted down another note, more thoughtful this time.

Daniella shifted uneasily.

Bowman caught it instantly.

"Let me be clear," he said, voice lowering. "I'm not here to judge whatever is going on between you two."

"We're not—" Russell started.

Bowman raised a hand. "Save it. I don't need the soap opera. I need the timeline."

Russell swallowed.

Daniella flushed.

Bowman continued, tone cooling. "Ashling's car didn't end up here by accident. Someone left it. Or lured her here. Or staged the whole scene. And the fact that she appears in your photos suggests she was watching you."

He held the print up again.

"Looking into the lens like she knew she needed to be seen."

Russell looked sick. Daniella looked pale.

Bowman leaned against the railing, staring at the water. "I've seen cases like this, Kane. People vanish for different reasons. Fear. Debt. Secrets. Threats."

He looked over his shoulder.

"But this? This one feels different."

"How?" Daniella asked quietly.

Bowman studied the scarf tied to the guardrail. "Because Ashling didn't leave a mess behind. She left a breadcrumb trail."

"Breadcrumbs?" Russell echoed.

Bowman nodded. "She wanted someone to follow the clues. And she wanted those clues to point in a specific direction. Which means she planned her disappearance—or she anticipated being taken."

Russell choked on his breath. "Taken? By who?"

Bowman didn't answer.

Not yet.

The detective walked to the front of the car, crouching beside the tire tracks left in the muddy shoulder.

"Kane," he called, motioning Russell forward. "Take a look here."

Russell joined him, reluctantly.

"Notice anything?" Bowman asked.

Russell squinted. "Just her tire tread."

"And that," Bowman said, pointing to a second imprint. "Another vehicle pulled up beside her."

Daniella gasped. "Someone else was here?"

"Recently," Bowman said. "Maybe the night she disappeared."

Russell's face drained of color.

Bowman stood slowly, brushing mud from his hands. "And that's not the only thing."

"What else?" Daniella asked.

Bowman pointed to faint footprints along the edge of the dam — too large to be Ashling's, spaced farther apart, leading toward the tree line and then disappearing into the forest.

Someone had walked here. Someone watching. Someone waiting.

Bowman rubbed his jaw. "We're dealing with someone clever. Someone precise. Someone who knows how to cover their tracks."

"Who would follow her?" Russell asked.

Bowman hesitated.

Then he said the thing they'd both been avoiding:

"Someone from her past."

Daniella felt a chill ripple down her spine.

Russell shook his head. "No. Ashling has never—"

"Yes," Bowman interrupted. "She has. I just didn't have enough to confront you with yet."

He pulled a thin manila file from his jacket.

It was labeled: A. MOORE — RESTRICTED.

Russell stared at it. "What is that?"

"A glimpse into a life your fiancée never told you about," Bowman said.

Russell reached for it—Bowman pulled it back.

"You see this," he warned, "you can't unsee it."

Russell's jaw clenched. "Show me."

Bowman glanced at Daniella. "You too. If you're part of this now, you need to know what she was mixed up in."

Daniella nodded shakily.

Bowman opened the file just enough for them to see the first page.

It wasn't a résumé.

Or a criminal record.

Or a medical report.

It was a classification form.

Central Intelligence Agency

Field Operative Registration

MOORE, ASHLING – Status: ACTIVE (RESTRICTED)

Reactivation Eligible: RIO Protocol

Daniella's breath vanished.

Russell staggered back as if someone punched him. "What… what the hell is this?"

Bowman's voice was low. "Ashling didn't work at a marketing firm. She didn't quit a job in the city for a quiet life. She was a trained operative. And her file resurfaced last week."

Russell's voice cracked. "She lied to me."

"She lied to everyone," Bowman said gently. "But maybe for good reason."

Daniella whispered, "She thought someone was after her."

Bowman nodded. "Someone is."

The detective snapped the file shut.

"And from what I can tell," he added, "Ashling Moore didn't disappear by choice."

He looked between them, his voice grave.

"She was pulled back into a classified operation."

"And now," Bowman said, "whoever wanted her… knows about both of you."

Later in the day, after endless interviews and circulating rumors, the crowd at the dam began to thin. Officers taped off the area, promising to resume the search at first light.

Russell remained near the railing long after sunset's glow faded. Daniella stood beside him. Neither spoke.

The water below roared in the gathering dark.

Finally, Russell whispered, "I don't know what's real anymore."

Daniella gently threaded her fingers through his. He squeezed tightly, the tension in him vibrating through her palm.

"You're real," she whispered. "Whatever she was… whatever she hid… You are still you."

He closed his eyes, breathing in deeply.

"And you," he whispered. "You're real too. The only thing

that makes sense right now."

She didn't let go.

Not when he trembled.

Not when he sagged slightly toward her.

Not when he whispered, "Stay with me tonight. Please."

She nodded.

And he exhaled — not because he was relieved, but because letting go hurt too much.

But across the dam, hidden in the dense woods, someone watched them through a long-range scope.

A mechanical click sounded as the watcher adjusted the focus, tracking Russell and Daniella as they walked toward her car.

A gloved hand scribbled in a small notebook.

Subjects converged. Emotional vulnerability exploited. Phase progression is optimal.

The notebook shut.

A cold smile formed behind the scope.

Ashling Moore wasn't the only ghost near Rio Dam. And some ghosts weren't interested in staying silent.

CHAPTER 9 – ALIBIS AND GUILT

The precinct smelled like stale coffee, paper, and fear.

Daniella had never been inside a detective's interview room before, but she had seen enough crime documentaries to know that everything inside these walls was designed to make a person uncomfortable. The metal table was too cold. The fluorescent lights were too bright. The ticking clock on the wall was too loud.

And the silence between her and Russell was too fragile.

Detective Mike Bowman sat on the opposite side of the table, his expression impossible to read. His strong fingers tapped rhythmically on the manila folder containing Ashling's classified file — a sound that struck Daniella's nerves like a slow, deliberate heartbeat.

"Let's start from the top," Bowman said. "Again."

"We've already told you—" Russell began, voice fraying.

"And you'll tell me again," Bowman said calmly. "Because nothing about this is simple. People who vanish rarely are."

Daniella tried to steady her breathing. Russell looked like he hadn't slept in days. His hair was mussed, jaw shadowed with stubble, eyes darkened from exhaustion and fear. When their legs brushed under the table, he didn't pull away...

But she did.

She needed clarity, not temptation.

"Daniella," Bowman said, pulling her back into the moment, "walk me through every interaction you've had with Ashling — from the moment you met her."

She swallowed. "We met at a café. She was… calm. Too calm. But the smile never reached her eyes."

"Most don't," Bowman muttered. "Continue."

"She said she'd seen my work," Daniella said.

"Compliment?" Bowman asked.

"Warning," Daniella replied.

Russell stiffened, remembering it too.

Bowman jotted a note. "She threatened you?"

"No," Daniella said truthfully. "Not directly. But she didn't like that Russell and I were working together. Or… how close we were sitting."

Russell flushed faintly.

Bowman's eyes flicked to him. "Did you have anything to hide?"

"We weren't—" Russell started.

Bowman raised a brow. "Weren't what?"

Daniella shifted in her seat. "We weren't involved romantically."

Bowman snorted. "Didn't ask if you were involved. I asked if you had something to hide."

Silence settled.

Daniella and Russell exchanged a look. A long one. A guilty one.

Bowman leaned back in his chair. "That's what I thought."

When it was Russell's turn, Bowman's tone hardened.

"Kane," he said, sliding the folder toward him. "Let's talk about your fiancée."

Russell's throat bobbed. "She wasn't... she wasn't who I thought she was."

"No," Bowman agreed. "She wasn't."

Russell clenched his fists. "Did you know? Before all this?"

"Some," Bowman admitted. "Not everything. But I had suspicions."

Russell's voice rose. "And you didn't tell me?"

"You wouldn't have believed me."

Daniella gently touched Russell's arm. "He's right."

He looked down at her hand, and for a brief moment, the world shrank to just their connection — a silent comfort amidst the storm.

Bowman noticed.

"You two close?" he asked casually.

Russell shot him a sharp look. "She's helping me."

"That's not what I asked."

Daniella pulled her hand away, heat climbing her neck.

"We're not—" she began.

Bowman waved her off. "Save the denials. They're boring. I deal in facts, and here are the facts: Ashling disappears. You two grow closer. Someone starts following you. Someone starts watching your studio. Someone sends you messages telling you to stop."

His stare was razor sharp.

"None of that happens by coincidence."

Daniella's fingers twisted together in her lap. Russell leaned back, rubbing his eyes.

"So what are you saying?" Russell asked.

"I'm saying," Bowman replied, "that Ashling was involved with something bigger than both of you. Something that puts you at risk. Something that makes your sudden closeness look... suspicious."

Russell's jaw tightened. "We're not suspects."

"Everyone is a suspect," Bowman said calmly. "Until I know who took her... or why she ran."

Daniella's stomach twisted.

"Detective," she said quietly, "Ashling wasn't jealous. She wasn't suspicious of Russell. She wasn't trying to intimidate me. She was trying to warn me."

Bowman's brows lifted. "Warn you?"

Daniella nodded. "She said I shouldn't read her thoughts. She said 'be careful.' She said we 'never know what we'll find near the dam.'"

Bowman tapped his pen again. "Cryptic."

"Intentional," Daniella said.

Russell looked between them, face pale. "Do you think she knew someone was coming for her?"

Bowman's jaw tightened. "I think she knew a lot more than she ever told you."

When the interview ended, Bowman stepped outside the room, leaving them alone.

The door clicked shut.

Russell exhaled shakily, rubbing his temples. "This is a nightmare."

Daniella shifted her chair closer. "I know."

He looked at her, really looked — eyes glassy with exhaustion, fear, and something softer.

"You shouldn't be dragged into this," he whispered.

"You didn't drag me into anything."

He shook his head. "I did. If you hadn't met me—"

"If I hadn't met you," she whispered, "I'd still be taking photos alone in a studio. I'm not going anywhere."

Emotion crossed his face, too raw for words.

He took her hand — not accidentally, not in passing, but deliberately.

His fingers wove through hers, slow and certain.

"I need you," he admitted quietly.

Her pulse stumbled.

Dangerous words. Forbidden words. Words spoken by a man whose fiancée's fate was still unknown.

But she didn't let go.

"Russell," she whispered, "you're not alone."

He leaned forward.

She leaned forward too.

Their breaths mingled... warm... trembling...

But before their lips could meet—

Bowman opened the door.

The sound was abrupt, loud, jarring.

They jerked apart instantly.

Bowman raised a brow. "Uh-huh. Thought so."

Daniella flushed scarlet. Russell looked away, jaw clenching.

Bowman tossed two cups of coffee on the table. "Drink. You'll need it."

Russell glared. "You could've knocked."

"I did," Bowman lied easily, sinking into his chair. "You two were just too busy making eyes at each other to hear it."

Daniella turned even redder. "We weren't—"

"Don't care," Bowman said, waving her off. "What I do care about is this."

He slid two envelopes toward them.

"Anonymous tip. Just came in."

Russell opened the first.

Inside:

A single photograph of Ashling standing near the dam.

Timestamped. Clear. Recent.

Daniella's breath caught. "She's alive."

Bowman nodded. "Looks that way."

Russell opened the second envelope.

Inside:

A photograph of them.

Daniella and Russell in her studio.

Taken through the window.

Daniella gasped. Russell's entire body went rigid.

"Someone's inside her building?" he demanded.

Bowman took the photo back calmly. "Someone's watching you."

Daniella shivered. "Why?"

Bowman stood.

His voice was low. Measured. Final.

"Because," he said, "Ashling Moore wasn't the only operative."

Daniella blinked. "What?"

Bowman held their eyes.

"And whoever she was running from... thinks you know something she didn't want anyone else to discover."

A cold dread seeped into Daniella's bones.

"What do they think we know?" she whispered.

Bowman stepped closer.

"That," he said quietly, "is what you need to find out before they get to you."

When Daniella and Russell left the precinct, rain had begun again — soft, cold droplets that kissed the pavement with muted taps.

Russell leaned against her car, closing his eyes, letting the rain cool his burning thoughts.

Daniella stood beside him, silent.

"There's something I need to tell you," he said finally.

Her heart thudded. "What?"

"When I look at you," he said softly, "I feel things I shouldn't feel. Not now. Not like this. Not with everything happening."

Her breath caught. "Russell—"

"But I can't shut it off," he whispered. His voice broke. "And I hate myself for it."

She stepped closer. "You shouldn't."

He shook his head violently. "Yes, I should. Ashling might be alive. She might be hurt. She might need me. And here I am—"

His voice faltered.

"Here you are what?" she breathed.

His answer was barely audible.

"Wanting you."

Her throat tightened.

"Russell," she whispered.

He pressed a hand over his eyes, exhaling shakily. "I shouldn't have said that."

"You should have," she said gently. "Because I feel it too."

His hand dropped.

Their eyes met — raw, longing, and terrified of what it meant.

His voice trembled. "What do we do?"

She placed her hand over his.

"Right now?" she whispered. "We survive."

He stared at her like she was the only thing keeping him grounded.

And in that moment, he wasn't wrong.

CHAPTER 10 — THE FIRST CRACK

The city felt different that night. Too quiet. Too watchful. Too aware.

Daniella sensed it the moment she stepped off the elevator and onto her floor — the flicker of the hallway light, the faint echo of footsteps that weren't hers, the way shadows seemed to cling to corners with unnatural patience.

She pushed open the door to her studio loft, her breath held tight in her chest.

Russell was already inside.

He sat on the worn leather couch near her window — elbows on his knees, hands threaded behind his neck, his whole body tense with something too heavy to carry alone.

The moment he looked up, everything inside her pulled toward him.

"Hey," she whispered.

He didn't answer at first.

He just studied her face — tired, vulnerable, searching for something he couldn't name yet.

She closed the door behind her. "You shouldn't be here alone."

He let out a raw, humorless laugh. "I'm never alone

anymore. Someone's always watching."

Her stomach tightened. "Bowman said he increased patrols around the area."

"Patrol isn't who's watching," he said, shaking his head. "It's whoever was tailing Ashling. Whoever sent those photos. Whoever knows where we were at the dam, where you shoot, where I park, what time we breathe—"

His voice broke.

Daniella crossed the room and knelt in front of him. "Russell."

He exhaled shakily. "I can't keep doing this."

Her hands gently cupped his jaw. "Look at me."

He did.

Slowly.

Painfully.

Like he was afraid he would crumble if he did it too soon.

"You're safe here," she whispered. "With me."

His breath stuttered. "Am I?"

"Yes."

He shook his head. "You can't guarantee that."

"I can guarantee I won't let you face this alone."

His eyes searched hers with desperate intensity. "Why? You barely know me."

"I know enough."

His voice lowered, raw. "Enough to risk everything?"

She leaned closer. "Enough to stand by you."

Her fingers grazed his cheek.

He closed his eyes, leaning into her touch like it was the first real comfort he'd felt in days.

"Daniella..." he breathed. "I'm not a good man right now."

"You're a man whose world just shattered," she whispered. "There's a difference."

His eyes opened — haunted, pleading, and burning.

"I don't know how to stop wanting you," he said.

Her pulse collided with her ribs.

"Then don't," she whispered.

Something in him broke.

The first crack.

Slow.

Quiet.

Inevitable.

He reached for her like gravity itself pulled him forward.

Their lips collided gently at first — a soft question, a trembling confession, a moment suspended between right and wrong.

Then the kiss deepened.

Hungry.

Delayed.

Fierce with emotion he'd been fighting for too long.

His hand slid into her hair, fingers threading through the strands as if memorizing the feel of her. She rose onto her knees, leaning into him, her own hands bracing against his chest.

He pulled her into his lap, breath hitching against her mouth.

"Tell me to stop," he whispered, forehead pressed to hers. "Tell me this is wrong."

"It's not," she whispered back. "It never was."

His lips found hers again — slow, searching, reverent.

But then—

BANG.

A noise outside the window.

They froze.

Another BANG.

Soft.

Deliberate.

Metallic.

Russell's hands tightened on her hips. Daniella's heart slammed against her ribs.

He stood abruptly, pulling her with him. "Stay behind me."

She obeyed.

He approached the window slowly… stepping closer… closer…

He peered outside.

Nothing.

Just the reflection of the streetlamp glistening off the damp fire escape. The faint hum of the city.

But he didn't relax.

Neither did she.

Daniella moved to the side of the window, peeking just enough to see the street below.

And then—

Her breath caught.

A man leaned against a black sedan across the street.

Dark jacket.

Hands in pockets.

Still. Too still.

He was staring directly at her building.

"Russell..." she whispered.

"I see him."

The man didn't move.

He didn't shift.

He just watched.

A cold shiver crawled up Daniella's spine. "Do we call Bowman?"

"Already did," Russell said, stepping back from the window. "He said someone would be here in ten minutes."

She swallowed hard. "Ten minutes is a long time."

Russell turned toward her — jaw tight, eyes blazing with fear and something else.

Determination.

He took her hands.

"You're not leaving my sight," he said.

She nodded.

He pulled her close — holding her tightly, grounding himself in her warmth, her presence, her heartbeat.

"I don't know what's happening," he whispered against her hair. "I feel like I'm losing my mind."

"You're not," she whispered. "You're surviving."

His fingers curled at her waist.

"I can't lose you," he said.

"You won't."

Thunder rumbled in the distance — the sky threatening another storm.

Russell tilted her chin up gently.

"We crossed a line tonight," he said softly.

"I know."

"I can't pretend I don't feel this anymore."

"I don't want you to."

He kissed her again — slower this time, aching, full of everything he didn't know how to say. She melted into him, hands gripping the back of his shirt, needing the connection just as desperately.

But then—

Footsteps echoed down the hallway outside the apartment.

Hard. Fast. Approaching.

Russell snapped into action. "Get back."

She grabbed her camera automatically — adrenaline sharpening her senses.

The footsteps stopped.

Right outside her door.

Silence.

Then—

A single, soft knock.

Not aggressive.

Not timid.

Measured.

Russell's voice hovered over a whisper. "Daniella... get behind me."

She did.

He approached the door, every muscle in his body tight with fear.

"Who is it?" Russell asked.

A voice answered on the other side — deep, calm, familiar.

"Bowman."

Daniella gasped in relief.

Russell opened the door quickly — tension snapping.

The detective stepped inside, rain dripping from the shoulders of his coat. His eyes scanned the room instantly, noting their closeness and the tension between them without comment.

"I saw the guy," he said. "He's gone."

"Did you follow him?" Russell asked.

Bowman shook his head. "He vanished. Like he knew every blind spot in this block."

Daniella shivered. "He was watching us."

"Yeah," Bowman said. "And that's a problem."

Russell clenched his jaw. "Who the hell is he? And why is he following us?"

Bowman wet his lips. "Because Ashling didn't disappear randomly. She was part of something called RIO Protocol. And now whoever was controlling her…"

He glanced between them.

"…wants you two next."

Daniella's stomach dropped.

Russell's breath stopped.

"Why us?" Daniella whispered.

Bowman stepped closer, voice low.

"Because she trusted you," he said. "And they can't afford that."

Daniella's breathing hitched.

Russell's hand found hers again, instinctively, protectively.

The detective's eyes locked onto their interlaced fingers.

"And because," he said slowly, "whatever relationship the two of you have… someone doesn't like it."

Daniella felt her pulse throb painfully.

Russell didn't let go.

Bowman sighed. "You two need to be careful. This isn't just a missing persons case anymore. It's a hunt. And you're in the middle of it."

The room fell into a chilling silence.

Outside, thunder rolled in again.

Inside, Daniella and Russell stood side by side — bonded by fear, desire, and a shared sense of something neither could name yet.

And somewhere outside, in the dark—

The watcher lit a cigarette.

Exhaled. Checked his phone.

Phase Two engaged.

A new message appeared beneath it.

A name. A photo. A target.

D. Russo

The watcher's cold smile returned.

And the danger wrapped tighter around them than either Daniella or Russell realized.

CHAPTER 11 – LINES CROSSED

The next morning, sunlight crept into Daniella's loft like a gentle intruder — soft, golden, tentative. It slipped across the hardwood floors, brushed the edges of her photography table, glowed against the framed cityscape prints she had hung on the wall.

It should have felt warm. Comforting. Safe.

But the moment Daniella opened her eyes, she knew nothing about today would be safe.

Russell lay asleep on the couch — or rather, sitting up with his head tilted back, still wearing last night's clothes. He had insisted on staying after Bowman left, claiming he didn't want her alone in the loft.

She suspected the truth:

He couldn't stand being alone with his thoughts.

And maybe... she didn't want to be alone with hers either.

She stood quietly, watching him for a moment.

He looked exhausted. Disheveled. Haunted.

But still beautiful in a way that made something warm curl in her chest.

She wrapped her arms around herself, trying to ground her racing thoughts.

This was dangerous. He was grieving.

Confused.

Vulnerable.

And she was becoming entangled in emotions she wasn't sure she could pull back from.

She turned toward the kitchen to make coffee, forcing herself to focus on something simple. But as she reached for the mugs, she felt him behind her.

Warm.

Close.

Silent.

She didn't turn.

Not yet.

He spoke first.

"You didn't sleep, did you?"

She exhaled slowly. "Maybe an hour."

He stepped closer — she felt the shift of air, the heat radiating off his chest. His voice was soft, rough, threaded with something unspoken.

"Every time I closed my eyes," he said, "I saw her. Not

Ashling. The man outside your building."

Her stomach tightened. "I know."

"He's watching us," Russell murmured. "Waiting."

"For what?" she whispered.

Russell's breath brushed her neck. "For one of us to slip."

She turned slowly in his arms, now face-to-face with him.

Close enough to feel the warmth of his breath.

Close enough to see the flicker in his hazel eyes — fear, longing, guilt, desire all twisted together.

"I hate this," Russell whispered. "I hate dragging you into something this dangerous."

"You didn't drag me," she said softly. "I chose to stay."

His jaw clenched. "Why?"

"Because..." She hesitated and lifted her chin, meeting his eyes. "Because when I'm with you, I don't feel alone. And I know you don't either."

He swallowed hard.

His hand lifted — slowly, gently — brushing a strand of hair behind her ear. His fingertips glided along her cheek, almost reverently.

"Daniella…" he breathed.

Her heartbeat stuttered.

"Yes?"

A long pause.

A trembling one.

Then—

"I shouldn't want you the way I do."

Her breath hitched. "But you do."

His eyes darkened. "More than I should admit."

She stepped closer.

Close enough for her body to brush his.

Close enough that the heat between them pulsed like a second heartbeat.

"Then don't admit it," she whispered. "Show me."

His resolve broke.

His hands slid to her waist, pulling her gently yet urgently against him.

Their lips met — a slow, deep kiss that tasted like confession and danger and everything they weren't allowed to feel.

He kissed her with hesitation at first — a man drowning in guilt — but she kissed him back with soft assurance, coaxing him to trust what was real in the moment between them.

He deepened the kiss, one hand cradling the back of her head, the other gripping her waist as if grounding himself.

"You make me forget everything," he murmured against her lips. "Even when I don't want to."

"You make me feel alive," she whispered. "Even when I shouldn't."

They kissed again — deeper, warmer, and closer— until both of them were breathless.

For a moment, it felt like the world had paused.

But then—

A cold realization cut through her chest.

"We can't do this," she breathed, pulling back slightly. "Not like this. Not when we don't know what happened to her."

His forehead rested against hers. "I know. I know."

But neither of them stepped away.

Neither could.

Their breaths mingled in the small space between them.

He finally opened his eyes, searching hers. "Tell me you feel this too."

She exhaled shakily. "I do."

"And tell me it's wrong."

She shook her head. "I can't."

His thumb brushed her lower lip, slow and soft. "Neither can I."

It was the first honest sentence either of them had spoken all morning.

They were about to speak again when—

THUD.

Something hit the outside of the loft door.

Daniella jumped.

Russell pushed her behind him instinctively. "Stay back."

Another THUD.

Slow.

Heavy.

Deliberate.

Russell's hand reached for her camera monopod — metal, sturdy, the closest thing to a weapon in the room.

He approached the door silently.

Daniella's heart slammed against her ribs.

Russell pressed his ear to the wood.

Silence. Then—

THUD.

LOUDER.

Daniella nearly gasped.

Russell motioned her toward the kitchen. "Call Bowman."

She grabbed her phone—but froze.

It vibrated first.

A text message.

UNKNOWN NUMBER

Her blood turned to ice.

She opened it.

A blurry photo.

Of her front door.

Taken from the hallway.

Russell saw her face pale. "What is it?"

She handed him the phone.

His jaw tightened. "He's here."

Suddenly—

Another text appeared.

Step outside. Alone.

Now.

Her hands trembled uncontrollably.

Russell grabbed her shoulders. "You are NOT going out there."

Another message:

Don't make me come in.

Daniella's breath shattered. "Russell..."

He pulled her into his chest protectively. "I'm not letting anything happen to you."

She felt his heartbeat — rapid, fierce, furious.

"Go to the back room," he whispered. "Lock the door."

"And you?" she whispered back.

His expression hardened. "I'm not leaving you. I'll stay between you and the door until Bowman gets here."

Before she could move—

The lights flickered.

Daniella gasped.

The building hummed.

Then clicked.

Then—

Darkness.

Complete and suffocating.

Russell grabbed her hand instantly. "Stay with me."

She pressed close as he guided her through the loft, careful, slow steps, his hand curled tightly around hers.

A faint glow from outside illuminated the window just enough for her to see the outline of his face — tense, jaw clenched, eyes searching the shadows.

They slipped into her small office at the back of the loft. Russell closed the door quietly and positioned himself against it.

Daniella pressed her back to the desk, trying to calm her racing heart.

"Bowman said there were blind spots in this building," Russell whispered. "The hallways. The stairwell."

She nodded, trembling. "You think he's out there right now."

"I know he is."

She swallowed hard. "Russell..."

He turned toward her — even in darkness, she saw the fear in his eyes.

And something stronger.

Promise.

"I'm not letting anything happen to you," he whispered fiercely. "I swear it."

She stepped closer, drawn to him like gravity itself.

Their bodies brushed.

Emotion swelled between them.

Fear.

Desire.

Connection.

Instinct.

His hand lifted — gently cupping her cheek in the dark.

"You're safe," he breathed. "I've got you."

She closed her eyes.

For a moment, she believed him.

But then—

The doorknob twisted.

Slowly. Silently.

Someone was trying to come in.

Russell froze.

Daniella's breath stopped.

The knob twisted again.

Then—

A soft voice through the door.

Male.

Cold.

Unfamiliar.

"Daniella… open the door."

Her body turned to stone.

Russell pressed her back, shielding her with his own body.

"Get behind me," he whispered.

She obeyed instantly.

"Open it," the voice repeated. "I won't ask again."

Russell's voice was low and deadly. "Leave us alone."

A long pause.

Then—

A whisper through the wood:

"You shouldn't have taken those pictures."

Daniella's blood ran cold.

Then footsteps moved away — slow, controlled — down the hall.

Russell didn't move until they faded completely.

He exhaled shakily. "We can't stay here."

Daniella grabbed his arm. "Where do we go?"

He looked at her — eyes burning.

"We go to Bowman. Now."

They fled the loft through the fire escape, descending three stories in cold morning air. Daniella's hands shook on the ladder.

Russell stayed behind her the entire time, one hand steady on her back, the other gripping the railing.

They reached the alley just as Bowman's unmarked sedan

screeched around the corner.

The detective threw open the door.

"Get in," Bowman barked. "Now."

They dove inside.

Bowman floored the gas.

"Who was outside?" Russell demanded. "We heard him."

Bowman didn't look away from the road. "Not who."

He tossed a file into the backseat.

"You need to see this."

Daniella opened it with shaking hands.

Inside were photographs.

Documents.

Surveillance notes.

And a name:

COLIN STRYKER

Former intelligence

Former field operative

Former handler...

...and directly tied to RIO Protocol.

Daniella's breath caught. "Why does this look like a dossier?"

Bowman's voice dropped.

"Because he's the man Ashling was running from."

Russell froze.

"And now," Bowman added grimly, "he's running toward you."

Daniella's pulse thundered in her ears.

Russell gripped her hand instinctively.

Lines had been crossed.

All of them.

And there was no going back.

CHAPTER 12 – SECRETS BENEATH THE SURFACE

Bowman's car sliced through the city streets like a dark bullet, tires hissing against the wet pavement. Morning fog clung to the windshield, swirling in ghostly patterns as the detective finally slowed enough to speak.

"Neither of you are safe at the loft," he said. "And I'm not taking you back to your place either, Kane. They know every location tied to either of you."

Russell's grip tightened around Daniella's hand. He hadn't let go once.

"Then where are we going?" he demanded.

Bowman's jaw flexed. "Somewhere they won't expect."

He took a sharp left, parking inside an underground garage beneath a defunct newspaper printing building. The enormous steel roll-up door groaned shut behind them.

Daniella stepped out of the car, heart thudding.

"This place is abandoned," she said quietly.

"Officially," Bowman replied, punching a security code into a hidden keypad on a concrete pillar. "Unofficially, it's where I do the work the department can't know about."

A heavy door slid open.

Inside was an unmarked operations room — dim lights

humming, screens lined across the walls, stacks of files, photographs, evidence bags. A scent of metal, old paper, and stale coffee hung in the air.

"This isn't just a missing person case," Bowman said, closing the door behind them. "This is a cover-up intersecting with an intelligence operation."

Daniella shivered. "We figured that part out."

Bowman motioned them closer to one of the monitors. "Not all of it."

The detective loaded a file onto the screen.

Grainy surveillance footage appeared — timestamped the night before.

A hallway.

A door.

Her door.

Daniella felt her knees weaken.

Russell gripped her waist, steadying her.

"That's the moment he stood outside your loft," Bowman said. "Your building's security cameras caught the tail end of it."

The figure on screen was tall.

Broad-shouldered.

Moving with calculated precision.

He wasn't nervous.

He wasn't rushing.

He was waiting.

Then the footage zoomed in.

His face wasn't fully visible — obscured by the hood of a dark jacket — but his jawline, posture, and stillness were enough to make Daniella's stomach twist.

"That's Stryker," Bowman said. "Former handler. Former operative. Former everything except what he is now."

"And what is that?" Russell asked tensely.

Bowman exhaled through his nose. "A ghost with unfinished business."

The footage jumped to another angle: the stairwell.

Stryker was walking down slowly.

Not hiding.

Then he paused at the landing.

Turned toward the camera.

And smirked.

Daniella gasped. "He knew he was being recorded."

"Exactly," Bowman said. "Which means this wasn't intimidation."

"It wasn't?" she whispered.

Bowman leaned in. "It was a message."

Russell's voice cracked. "What kind of message?"

Bowman turned to them both, face grave.

"That you're not alone in this investigation."

"And that he wants you to know it."

They moved into a smaller room filled with case boards. Photos of Ashling were pinned everywhere — alone, with Russell, walking through markets, stepping out of cafés, glancing over her shoulder on the subway.

"She was under surveillance long before she vanished," Bowman said.

Russell looked sick. "How long?"

Bowman flipped a page in the file. "Six months."

Daniella covered her mouth. "Six months?"

Russell staggered back, shaking his head. "She never said a word."

"Operatives rarely do," Bowman replied. "Especially when their enemies aren't amateurs."

On a second board were photos from Daniella's Rio Dam shoot.

Russell frowned. "You've already analyzed these?"

"I had them digitized," Bowman said. "Something about them bothered me."

He zoomed in on the shot with the mysterious second figure — barely visible behind a rock formation.

"Look here," Bowman said, enhancing the image.

The figure came into slightly sharper focus.

Daniella's breath caught.

It wasn't just a man.

It was Stryker.

Russell stiffened. "He was there that day?"

Bowman nodded. "Watching Ashling. Watching you. Watching Daniella."

He turned to face them.

"With how deeply he's embedded himself, I'd bet he knew about the shoot before you even got in the car."

Daniella felt a cold tremor ripple through her.

"But that doesn't explain this," Bowman added, pulling another photo off the board — a shot Daniella didn't remember taking.

"What is that?" she asked.

"Your camera took it," Bowman said. "Sometime between your last set of shots and when you packed up."

The image was blurry — movement or a sudden jerk — but one detail was unmistakable.

Ashling.

Running.

Face turned toward the lens.

Eyes wide with fear.

Mouth open in a scream that the camera couldn't capture.

"What the hell?" Russell whispered, voice cracking. "She never—"

"She never told you," Bowman finished. "Because she was protecting you."

"And now," Bowman said quietly, "she's protecting Daniella."

Daniella's breath vanished. "Me?"

Bowman nodded. "I think Ashling knew Stryker was watching her. And she knew you caught more in your photos than you realized."

"She left me out of it," Daniella whispered. "She didn't want me involved."

"She didn't have a choice," Bowman said. "And neither do you now."

Russell stepped in front of Daniella protectively. "She's not a part of this."

Bowman's stare was sharp. "She became part of this the moment Stryker stepped onto her floor last night."

Russell froze.

Daniella's chest tightened.

Bowman gestured toward another screen. "There's more."

Video footage began playing.

This time, from the alley behind Daniella's building.

The fire escape.

They watched themselves climbing down in the dark.

But within seconds—

Another figure slipped into the frame.

Stryker.

Standing beside Bowman's car.

Watching them.

Listening.

Waiting.

Daniella's heart twisted painfully.

"He was there," she whispered.

"He followed you the whole time," Bowman said. "He's not just tracking Ashling."

"He's tracking you."

Daniella swallowed hard. "Why me?"

Bowman hesitated — which terrified her more than anything.

"Because," he said slowly, "Ashling left something behind."

Russell's breath caught. "What?"

Bowman pointed to Daniella.

"With her."

They moved to a metal table covered with files. Bowman unlocked a drawer and pulled out a sealed evidence bag.

Inside it was an SD card.

Daniella blinked. "What is that?"

Bowman set it down carefully. "This was found in Ashling's car."

"My car?" Russell whispered, confused.

"No," Bowman said gently. "Her abandoned car at the dam."

Daniella stared. "And you think—"

"I don't think," Bowman interrupted. "I know."

He slid the bag toward her.

"There's only one name scribbled on the label."

Daniella's pulse thundered as she read it.

RUSSO

Her eyes widened. "She left this for me?"

Bowman nodded. "She trusted you to find what she couldn't say."

Russell exhaled sharply. "Why not give it to me? Why Daniella?"

Bowman's voice softened. "Because she didn't trust you to survive knowing what's on it."

Russell's entire body went rigid. "What the hell does that mean?"

"It means," Bowman said carefully, "that whatever Ashling uncovered... she realized you might be used to get to it."

Daniella covered her mouth. "Russell..."

Bowman held up a hand. "You two need to listen. Ashling was trying to protect both of you. Daniella — she trusted you to handle this information. Russell — she trusted you not to be compromised by it."

"Compromised?" Russell breathed.

"Love," Bowman said simply. "She knew you loved her. And she also saw the way you looked at Daniella."

Silence spread through the room like a stain.

Daniella's throat tightened. "Bowman..."

"She wasn't blind," he continued. "She knew your weakness. But she also knew Daniella's strength."

Russell shook his head. "This is insane."

Bowman leaned in. "No. This is survival."

He slid a laptop toward Daniella.

"You're opening the SD card."

She swallowed hard. "What if Stryker knows I have it?"

Bowman met her eyes.

"He does," he said. "That's why he's escalating."

Russell stepped in front of Daniella again, protective instinct blazing. "If she opens that card, she's a target."

"She already is," Bowman said.

Daniella steadied her breath.

"Do we know what's on it?" she asked.

Bowman shook his head. "Encrypted. Only one person can decrypt it."

"Who?" Russell demanded.

Bowman pointed at Daniella.

"You," he said. "Or Ashling wouldn't have left it for you."

Daniella stared at the SD card, every nerve in her body on fire.

Russell placed a hand on her shoulder — gentle, protective, warm.

"You don't have to do this," he murmured.

She lifted her eyes to his.

"Yes," she whispered. "I do."

Bowman nodded. "Then let's begin."

He placed the laptop in front of her.

Daniella slid the SD card into the port.

The screen flickered.

A loading bar appeared.

Russell squeezed her hand.

Then—

A single folder popped up.

R.I.O — Phase One

Bowman's face drained of color.

"Oh, hell."

Daniella double-clicked the folder.

A password prompt appeared.

Bowman leaned over her shoulder. "Try something she'd trust you to know."

Daniella swallowed.

A password.

Not for Russell.

Not for Bowman.

For her.

She typed slowly.

LENS

Rejected.

She tried again.

RUSSO

Rejected.

Bowman frowned. "She wouldn't make it obvious."

Russell stepped forward. "Try—"

He stopped.

His eyes widened.

Daniella's did too.

Ashling's last words to her at the café.

I hope you don't read mine.

Daniella typed:

THOUGHTS

The screen flickered.

Unlocked.

Russell gasped. "Holy—"

Then the files loaded.

Dozens of them.

Photos.

Voice recordings.

Encrypted messages.

Maps.

Coordinates.

Profiles.

Surveillance logs.

Bank accounts.

Operative names.

One folder stood out.

COLIN STRYKER — Handler Termination Order

Russell's breath hitched violently. "What does that mean?"

Bowman exhaled. "It means Ashling wasn't running from Stryker."

He looked at them both.

"She was assigned to take him out."

Daniella felt the room tilt.

"And she failed," Bowman added.

Russell closed his eyes.

"And now," Bowman finished quietly, "he's coming after the only people she trusted."

The air in the room grew cold.

Daniella looked at the files.

Ashling's secrets.

Ashling's escape.

Ashling's fear.

Ashling's plan.

Buried beneath the surface.

All of it leading here.

To this moment.

To them.

Russell grabbed Daniella's hand, squeezing tightly.

"We're in this together," he said.

She nodded.

But neither of them realized the truth:

The moment Daniella unlocked that folder—

Phase Two began.

And somewhere in the shadows, Stryker smiled.

CHAPTER 13 – THE BROTHER'S LIE

The rain had not stopped.

It came down in sheets across the Hudson Valley, drumming against the wide windows of Bowman's hidden operations room as afternoon melted into a bleak, bruised dusk. Thunder cracked low and distant, rolling through the concrete bowels of the abandoned building like the earth itself was shifting beneath their feet.

The discovery of the SD card had changed everything.

Daniella felt it — in the heaviness in her chest, the tremor in her fingertips, the way Russell kept reaching for her hand as if grounding himself. As if grounding her.

Bowman had gone quiet.

That was the worst sign of all.

He wasn't muttering.

Wasn't pacing.

Wasn't lecturing.

He stared at the decrypted files, jaw locked, eyes storm-dark.

Something inside that folder had rattled even him.

"Detective," Daniella said softly, stepping closer. "You haven't said anything in ten minutes."

Bowman didn't look up. "I'm reading."

"You're glaring," Russell countered. "And you only glare when something's bad."

"Everything in this damn file is bad," Bowman snapped, then dragged a hand down his face. "But this? This is worse."

He clicked on a highlighted document.

Daniella's stomach tightened.

Russell leaned in beside her, shoulder brushing hers.

The file displayed a timeline.

Names.

Movements.

Associations.

And at the top:

ASHLING MOORE – Asset Profile

Handler: Colin Stryker

Primary Contact: BRYAN JACOBS

Secondary Cover: RUSSELL KANE (Unaware)

Russell flinched as if struck.

"I was her cover?" he whispered.

Bowman nodded. "Ashling used you as a civilian stability anchor. It's not uncommon for operatives to appear engaged or married — it helps reduce suspicion."

Russell closed his eyes, pain slicing across his expression. "She never loved me."

Daniella reached for his hand. "Russ—"

He shook his head but tightened his fingers around hers instinctively.

Bowman clicked to the next page.

Bryan Jacobs – Brother or Handler?

Status: UNKNOWN

Role: CONFIDENTIAL

Last Known Communication: 11:52 p.m., the night before disappearance

Message Flagged: PRIORITY RED

Daniella frowned. "Bryan? What does he have to do with this?"

Bowman exhaled. "More than he's admitted."

Russell swallowed. "He lied to me. He told me Ashling stayed with him sometimes. That she was stressed, distant"

"Partially true," Bowman said. "But not why."

"What was the reason?" Daniella asked.

Bowman clicked play on a hidden audio clip.

The moment it began, Daniella felt her pulse spike.

A woman's voice.

Shaking.

Breathless.

Ashling.

"Bryan, listen to me. I don't have time. They found out."

A scraping sound. A shiver of panic.

"I can't run anymore. Not alone."

Russell tensed beside her.

Daniella squeezed his arm.

Ashling continued:

"If something happens... You know what to do. You know who to protect."

A pause.

A trembling inhale.

"Not Russell. He'll be used. Protect her."

The audio cracked.

Cut.

Ended.

Silence swallowed the room.

Russell staggered back. "Protect... her?"

His eyes flew to Daniella.

"Me?" she whispered.

"You," Bowman said. "Ashling wasn't afraid for herself. She was afraid for you."

"But why me?" Daniella asked, voice trembling.

Bowman looked at her with something like respect mixed with worry.

"Because you have something she didn't."

Daniella blinked. "Photography?"

"No," Bowman said. "Courage to dig. And the innocence of an outsider. Stryker can't predict you. You're not trained. You're not compromised. You're the one factor he didn't account for."

Daniella's mouth went dry. "And that makes me a threat?"

"To him," Bowman said. "Yes."

Russell moved instantly to her side, protective instinct flaring. "He's not touching her."

Bowman gave a grim nod. "That's going to be… difficult."

A harsh buzzing cut through the room.

Not Bowman's phone.

Not the computer.

Not the overhead lights.

A small emergency cell phone tucked into a metal drawer vibrated violently.

Bowman jerked it out.

"Only one person has this number," he muttered.

He answered.

"Bowman."

A faint voice crackled through the static.

Daniella's heart stopped.

Russell's breath caught.

It was Bryan.

Barely audible.

Panicked.

Broken.

"Detective... I messed up."

Bowman's tone went sharp. "Jacobs, where are you?"

"I—I don't know. A cabin. Woods. They dragged me here."

Russell froze. "Dragged? Bryan, what happened? Where's Ashling?"

Bowman waved him silent, keeping the line open.

Bryan's breathing hitched. "I lied. I lied to all of you."

Daniella swallowed. "About what?"

"About her disappearance," Bryan whispered. "About why she ran. About what she was hiding."

Russell stepped closer to the phone, voice cracking. "Bryan, talk to us!"

But Bryan's words tumbled out quickly, strained.

"I didn't help her disappear, Russell. I helped cover for her."

Russell's eyes widened. "Cover... what?"

Bowman stiffened, listening.

Bryan's voice fractured.

"I wasn't her brother."

The room went still.

Dead still.

Russell's face drained of color. "What... what are you talking about? Bryan, what are you—"

"I'm not her brother," Bryan choked out. "I was her partner."

Daniella's pulse slammed into her ribs.

"Partner?" she whispered.

Bowman's jaw tightened. "In the field. A paired operative."

The truth hit like a blade.

Russell staggered back, shaking his head. "No. She told me he was her brother. They grew up together. They—"

"They lied," Bowman said softly.

Bryan's voice crackled through the phone again.

"It was my job to watch her. To protect her. To keep her cover intact. She needed a civilian tie — that was you, Russell — but I was her handler in the field."

The betrayal cut deeper than any blade.

Russell's hands shook violently.

"I didn't know," Bryan whispered. "She didn't tell me everything. She only told me enough to keep you safe."

Russell whispered, "She used me."

Bryan's voice cracked. "She loved you, Russell. Maybe not the way you wanted — but she did. And she trusted you. But she didn't trust the Agency. And she didn't trust Stryker."

Daniella felt the room tilt.

"What was she running from?" she asked.

Bryan exhaled shakily.

"She discovered something. Something Stryker hid from the Agency. Something that turned him rogue."

Daniella leaned closer. "What did she find?"

Bryan's voice dropped.

"Files. Names. One in particular."

Bowman tensed. "Who?"

The phone crackled violently with static.

Bryan spoke one word before the line cut:

"Yours."

Bowman froze.

Russell's breath stopped.

Daniella stared.

The phone went dead.

Bowman lowered it slowly, expression unreadable.

"Detective?" Daniella whispered. "What did he mean by yours?"

Bowman didn't answer.

Not right away.

He turned away from them, fists clenching once, twice, shoulders rising and falling with the force of a man choking on a truth he never wanted to see light.

Finally, he spoke.

"I knew Ashling," Bowman said quietly. "Before the dam. Before Russell. Before any of this."

Russell flinched. "What?"

Bowman turned, face grave.

"She didn't vanish into the Agency alone," he said. "I was her oversight contact. Her cross-agency liaison."

Daniella's heart hammered. "You were working with her?"

"Yes."

"And you didn't tell us?" Russell snapped.

"It was classified."

"She died because of classified secrets!" Russell shouted.

"She isn't dead," Bowman said sharply.

Silence.

Heavy.

Suffocating.

Charged.

Bowman stepped closer to them.

"I didn't tell you because I didn't know which side she was on anymore. Whether she was compromised." His voice tightened. "Or whether I was."

Daniella's breath froze. "Stryker turned rogue. What if he wasn't working alone?"

Bowman nodded slowly.

"He wasn't."

The air in the room grew colder.

Russell swallowed hard. "Are you telling us someone inside the Agency wants us dead?"

Bowman lifted his eyes.

Not cold.

Not detached.

But haunted.

"Yes," he said. "And we need to find Ashling before they find you."

A sharp, violent noise cracked through the hallway —

BANG.

Then another.

BANG.

Footsteps.

Fast.

Heavy.

Approaching the operations room.

Bowman grabbed his gun, motioning them behind a metal filing cabinet.

"Stay down," he hissed.

Daniella grabbed Russell's arm.

Russell pulled her tight against his chest, turning her away from the door.

The footsteps stopped outside.

Silence.

Then a low voice:

"Detective."

Bowman stiffened.

"That you, old friend?"

Bowman's face blanched.

He knew the voice.

Russell whispered, "Who is that?"

Bowman whispered back:

"Stryker."

Daniella's blood iced.

Stryker's voice curled through the door like smoke.

"We need to talk."

Bowman stood slowly, weapon raised.

Russell's grip tightened on Daniella's waist.

Her heart slammed against his chest.

Stryker spoke one last time.

Calm.

Chilling.

Certain.

"You can't keep them from me forever. You know that."

Then—

Footsteps receded.

Fast.

Gone.

Bowman waited ten seconds before lowering his weapon.

"Pack everything," he said, voice rigid with urgency. "We're leaving. Now."

Russell helped Daniella to her feet.

"What's happening?" she whispered.

Bowman grimaced. "The Brother lied."

Daniella swallowed. "About what?"

Bowman's eyes hardened.

"About Ashling's disappearance."

He met their eyes with quiet gravity.

"She didn't vanish."

A beat of silence.

"She was taken."

And for the first time since the case began,

Bowman looked afraid.

CHAPTER 14 – BETWEEN LIGHT AND SHADOW

Night swallowed the abandoned printing building by the time they emerged — the kind of thick, heavy darkness that made every shadow feel alive. The air outside was damp, tinged with rain and the metallic scent of the Hudson drifting through the valley.

Bowman hustled them toward his unmarked car, scanning every rooftop, every alleyway, every blind corner like a man who suddenly felt the crosshairs lining up on his back.

Because they were.

"Stryker can't be far," Bowman muttered. "He wouldn't announce himself unless he wanted pressure on us."

Russell placed a steady hand on Daniella's back as they hurried toward the car. His touch was protective, warm, grounding. She leaned into it instinctively.

Bowman caught the gesture but said nothing — his silence loud, loaded.

Inside the vehicle, the tension pressed in on all three of them.

The detective drove with one hand on the wheel, the other hovering near the weapon holstered at his hip.

"Detective," Daniella finally said, voice small but steady, "You need to tell us the rest."

Bowman didn't pretend to misunderstand. He inhaled deeply, exhaling through gritted teeth.

"There's no rest to tell," he said. "Only pieces. I'm still assembling the picture."

Russell leaned forward, voice tight with frustration. "You knew Ashling before I did. That wasn't just liaison stuff. What aren't you telling us?"

Bowman's eyes flicked to the rearview mirror. "Drop it."

"No." Russell's voice rose. "Not this time."

Bowman's jaw tightened. "Not now."

"When?" Russell snapped. "When one of us ends up like her? Missing? Dragged into the woods? What else did she tell you that you're hiding?"

Bowman slammed the brakes.

The car skidded to a halt on an empty back road, rain streaking across the windshield.

Daniella gasped, bracing her hands against the dashboard.

Russell whipped his head toward her, instantly checking her. "You okay?"

She nodded shakily.

Bowman turned in his seat, face shadowed but fierce.

"You think you want the truth?" he asked Russell. "Fine. Here it is."

Thunder echoed in the distance.

"I met Ashling long before she met you. Before the agency burned her. Before Stryker turned."

Daniella leaned in, pulse quickening.

Bowman continued, "She wasn't just an operative. She was my informant."

Russell froze. "Informant?"

"She fed me intel from inside RIO Protocol. Intel on Stryker. Intel on black ops that the Agency denied existed. Intel on things people have been killed for whispering about."

Daniella shivered. "So she trusted you."

Bowman let out a bitter laugh. "No. She used me, too. They all do."

He rubbed a hand over his face.

"But she warned me of one thing. One thing only."

"What?" Russell asked.

Bowman's eyes lifted, dark and haunted.

"She said the next target wouldn't be her."

He pointed at Daniella.

"She said it would be you."

Daniella's breath hitched. "Me?"

Bowman nodded.

"She said you'd be targeted because you weren't part of their world. Because you'd see things no operative would risk noticing. Because you'd capture things no one else could."

Daniella's throat tightened. "With my camera."

"With your instincts," Bowman corrected. "Your compassion. Your timing. Your access."

Russell reached for her hand, his voice a rasp. "She was protecting you even then."

Daniella swallowed hard. "But I didn't know her."

Bowman nodded slowly. "Doesn't matter. She knew you."

Lightning flashed, illuminating his expression.

"Ashling never told me why. But she said you were the one person she couldn't risk Stryker getting near."

"But he did," Russell whispered. "He was at her building. At the dam. Outside her studio."

"And inside the stairwell," Bowman added. "Footsteps don't lie."

Daniella felt nausea twist through her stomach. "Why does he want me?"

Bowman hesitated.

"Because Ashling left something with you," he said quietly. "Something bigger than the SD card."

Russell turned to her sharply. "What?"

Daniella shook her head. "I don't understand—"

Bowman started driving again, his tone clipped. "You will."

They arrived at Rio Dam just as the storm paused, dark clouds drifting in bruised purples and blacks across the sky. The air was thick with mist, swirling across the water like breath on a mirror.

The dam's lights flickered weakly, casting eerie reflections across the rushing spillway.

Russell stepped out first, scanning the tree line like he expected Stryker to lunge from the shadows.

"Why are we here?" he demanded.

Bowman stood beside him, rain dripping from his coat's collar. "Because this is where it started. And it's where it'll end."

Daniella followed them toward the guardrail where Ashling's scarf had once fluttered.

The scent of wet earth and Cold River rose around them.

Bowman pulled a flashlight from his pocket and aimed it down the rocky embankment.

"This is where her car was found," he said. "This is where she left the SD card in the glove box. This is where she led the Agency."

He paused.

"And this is where she underestimated Stryker."

Russell's jaw clenched. "How do you know that?"

Bowman stepped over the railing.

"Because someone left this."

He held up a thin, black object.

Daniella gasped. "A flash drive?"

Bowman nodded. "Found wedged between rocks. Dry. Wrapped in a waterproof casing. Placed intentionally."

Russell exhaled sharply. "Ashling."

"Or Stryker," Bowman countered. "Either way, this is meant for you."

"For me?" Daniella whispered.

Bowman nodded. "You're the only one he hasn't confronted directly. Until last night."

Russell flinched, stepping in closer to her automatically.

"Let's get inside," Bowman said. "We're too exposed out here."

They hurried to a maintenance shed by the dam — dusty, cold, filled with old tools and the faint scent of oil.

Bowman closed the door behind them and locked it.

Russell stayed beside Daniella, arm brushing hers protectively.

Bowman placed the flash drive on a small wooden table and plugged it into his field laptop.

The screen blinked.

Loaded.

Opened one folder.

Just one.

Labeled:

RUSSO-14

Daniella's breath trembled. "My name again."

Russell took her hand, threading their fingers tightly.

Bowman clicked.

A single video file appeared.

He opened it.

Static filled the screen.

Then—

A woman's face came into view.

Wet hair.

Wind-whipped.

Eyes wide with fear.

Breathing fast.

Ashling.

Daniella choked on air. "Oh my God."

Russell stepped closer to the screen, seeing her alive on the dam — terrified, but alive.

Ashling spoke into the camera, voice cracking.

"If you're seeing this... they found me."

Russell's breath broke.

"Daniella... listen to me."

Daniella nearly collapsed.

Ashling knew her.

She knew her name.

She was speaking directly to her.

Russell steadied her by her waist.

Ashling continued:

"Everything you think you know… is wrong. Stryker wasn't coming for me."

Her eyes darted around the frame.

"He was coming for you."

Daniella covered her mouth.

Russell whispered, "What? Why?"

Ashling swallowed hard.

"Because you saw something. You photographed something. Something I failed to capture."

Bowman froze.

Ashling's voice shook violently.

"Stryker killed someone. At this dam. Someone the Agency buried. Someone whose existence ruins everything RIO Protocol was built on."

Daniella's heart pounded so hard she thought her ribs would crack.

Ashling leaned closer to the camera.

"And you photographed the proof."

Russell stared at Daniella, stunned. "You what?"

Daniella shook her head wildly. "I—I didn't know—"

Ashling's voice cut through the panic.

"Daniella, listen. They bury bodies in these waters. Operatives who turn. Civilians who know too much. Assets that outlive their use."

Russell held onto Daniella tighter.

Ashling's expression shattered.

"Stryker killed one of them. I saw the aftermath. You caught the moment."

Bowman's breath hitched. "She's talking about a black operation."

Ashling looked into the camera with desperate intensity.

"Whatever is in your photos... whatever you captured... It's the evidence they've been trying to destroy for years."

Lightning flashed outside.

Ashling's final words came fast, panicked:

"Don't trust anyone. Not the Agency. Not RIO. Not even—"

The video glitched.

Static.

Then—

A single image appeared before the screen went black.

One frame.

One photograph.

One horrifying revelation—

A man lying on the rocks below the dam.

Motionless.

Face half-submerged.

A bullet wound in his skull.

A hand gripping the back of his head.

A shadow standing behind him.

A shape Daniella recognized.

The silhouette from the edges of her photos.

Stryker.

Russell gasped. "Daniella... you photographed a murder."

Bowman whispered, "No."

His voice carried horror.

"Stryker wasn't killing a civilian."

He zoomed the image.

Daniella's breath shattered.

The dead man...

Had a badge clipped to his belt.

A badge from the same agency Ashling belonged to.

Bowman's voice dropped into a whisper of disbelief.

"He killed a federal agent."

Lightning cracked.

The shed went dark.

And from outside the door—

A soft, chilling sound.

Footsteps.

Slow.

Purposeful.

Getting closer.

Russell pulled Daniella behind him.

Bowman drew his gun.

Daniella's heart raced so violently she couldn't breathe.

Then—

A voice slid through the crack beneath the door.

Calm.

Cold.

Familiar.

"Daniella... open the door."

Stryker.

He was here.

At the dam.

At the shed.

At their door.

Russell's hand closed over Daniella's.

"We're not opening anything," Russell hissed.

Stryker chuckled quietly.

"Then I'll let myself in."

The doorknob began to turn.

Bowman raised his weapon.

Russell wrapped an arm around Daniella, pulling her against him.

Daniella's breath trembled.

Everything was about to shatter.

Between light and shadow—

They were no longer safe.

Not anywhere.

And Stryker had just found them.

CHAPTER 15 — BREAKING POINT

The shed door jolted violently in its frame.

The metal hinges groaned. Dust shook loose from the ceiling. Daniella's breath caught in her throat, her body pressed tightly against Russell's as the knob twisted inch by inch.

He was coming in.

Bowman raised his gun with a steady arm, but the tension in his jaw betrayed the truth — he wasn't sure if even a bullet would stop Colin Stryker.

"Stryker!" Bowman barked. "Back away from the door."

A low, cold chuckle slid through the crack beneath the threshold.

"You know I can't do that, Detective."

Russell's arm tightened protectively around Daniella's waist. She clung to him, heart pounding so violently she could barely hear anything else.

"Daniella," Stryker said, his voice smooth and intimate, as though they were standing inches apart instead of a door away. "Open up."

She shook her head quickly, whispering into Russell's chest, "No. No."

Russell pressed a kiss to the top of her head — instinct, desperation, maybe even love — and whispered, "I've got you. I swear."

Stryker tapped a knuckle against the metal.

Clink. Clink. Clink.

Slow.

Measured.

Taunting.

"You found the video, didn't you?" he called. "Ashling was always too clever. Too emotional. Too reckless."

Russell snarled. "If you touched her—"

Stryker chuckled. "Oh, Russell. Sweet, naïve Russell. You were her cover. Not her partner."

Russell lunged toward the door, but Bowman grabbed him by the collar and yanked him back.

"Don't," Bowman hissed. "That's what he wants."

The doorknob stopped turning.

A quiet moment passed.

Then Stryker said something that made Daniella's blood freeze solid.

"You took the photograph that ruined everything."

Russell stiffened.

Bowman cursed under his breath.

Daniella's knees buckled.

Stryker continued, voice calm as death.

"The photograph that showed me killing an agent. The photograph that exposes the RIO Protocol. The photograph shows Ashling died trying to get to you."

Daniella's pulse stopped. "Died...?"

Bowman threw his arm out, silencing her.

But Stryker heard the catch in Daniella's voice.

"Oh, she's alive," Stryker said. "Somewhere. For now. But she made the mistake of trusting you to keep her secret."

A metallic click sounded.

A lock releasing.

Bowman went white.

"He has a key," he whispered.

Russell held Daniella behind him, trembling with rage. "How the hell—?"

"Operatives have access to all federal maintenance

buildings around classified zones," Bowman snapped. "It's part of site control!"

The lock clicked again.

Another turn.

Another inch.

Bowman leaned in and whispered, "When I tell you to run, you run."

Daniella's breath shattered. "Where?"

"I'll buy you time."

"No!" Russell snapped. "He'll kill you."

"He already tried," Bowman muttered. "And he'll try again. But he wants the girl first."

Daniella whimpered. Russell pulled her tighter.

The final lock slid.

The metal bolt clacked.

The door began to swing inward—

—and Bowman smoked the light switch.

The shed plunged into total darkness.

"RUN!" Bowman shouted.

Russell grabbed Daniella, hauling her toward the back exit just as a silenced bullet pinged into the metal wall beside them.

Pfft.

Pfft.

Pfft.

Gunfire in the dark.

Bowman dove behind a workbench.

"Go!" he roared. "Go!"

Russell kicked open the back door, dragging Daniella into the freezing rain outside. Mud splashed beneath their feet as they tore down the embankment.

Behind them—

Stryker's silhouette filled the doorway.

Tall.

Still.

Deadly.

A flash of lightning lit the sky — illuminating his weapon raised, pointed directly at Daniella's spine.

"DOWN!" Russell yelled, tackling her to the ground as a

bullet ripped past them.

The grass splintered.

The river roared.

Thunder swallowed the night.

They scrambled behind a large boulder just as Stryker stepped into the open, stalking them with the calm patience of a man who had hunted for years.

"Come out, Daniella," he called. "I only need you alive."

Russell hissed under his breath, "Not helping."

Another silenced shot pinged against the rock.

"You see?" Stryker shouted. "Russell can die. Bowman can die. But you... You're necessary."

Daniella shivered violently. Russell snarled, cupping her face in his hands.

"Listen to me," he whispered fiercely, shaking with adrenaline. "I will die before I let him touch you."

She grabbed his shirt, voice trembling. "Don't say that."

He kissed her forehead, desperate and fierce.

He didn't say "I love you."

He didn't need to.

It was in his eyes — wild, terrified, real.

Stryker's footsteps drew closer on the wet brush.

Russell pulled her tighter, pressing her to his body, whispering low, "When I run left, you run right."

"What? No!"

"That's the only way one of us survives."

"We survive together!" she whispered fiercely.

He shook his head.

His thumb brushed her cheek in the rain.

He was about to sacrifice himself.

She realized it instantly.

And she snapped.

"If you run out there and let him kill you," she whispered fiercely, grabbing his jacket, "I will never forgive you."

His breath caught.

Her tears mixed with the rain.

"And I know you feel it too," she whispered. "I know what last night was. I know what we are. Don't you dare throw that away."

Russell closed his eyes, jaw clenched with emotion and

agony.

But Stryker's voice cut through their moment like a knife.

"You can't hide from me forever," he called. "I can see your heat signatures from here."

Russell looked at Daniella.

Then—

He kissed her.

Hard.

Deep.

Desperate.

A kiss that said everything they had been holding back — fear, longing, love, and terror all twisted into one breakable moment.

"Stay behind me," he whispered against her lips.

Her tears fell.

He turned, bracing himself.

But before he could move—

A deafening CRACK cut through the storm.

Bowman.

From the hill above.

He had his weapon raised.

"HEY, ASSHOLE!" Bowman bellowed over the thunder.

Stryker pivoted.

Bowman fired.

The bullet sparked against Stryker's shoulder.

He staggered back, expression shifting from cold confidence to fury.

"You just made a mistake!" Stryker snarled.

Bowman fired again.

This time, the bullet grazed Stryker's leg.

Stryker hissed, stumbling slightly — but he didn't fall.

He aimed at Bowman.

Russell grabbed Daniella.

"MOVE!"

They sprinted along the dam's edge as Stryker and Bowman exchanged rapid fire.

Bullets bit into the rocks.

Thunder cracked.

The river roared beneath them.

Russell yanked Daniella toward a maintenance stairwell.

"Down here!"

They descended fast, boots slipping on the rain-slicked metal steps.

Behind them, Stryker stopped firing.

Silence fell.

Too sudden.

Too wrong.

Russell froze.

Daniella froze against him, her chest heaving.

Bowman's distant voice echoed through the storm.

"Where the hell did he—"

A gunshot.

Bowman's voice cut off.

Daniella gasped.

"NO!" she cried.

Russell pulled her down the last steps, shoving her behind a concrete pillar. "Stay down!"

Her heart pounded in her ears.

Rain soaked her clothes.

Her hair clung to her face.

Her hands trembled uncontrollably.

Stryker's voice slipped through the rain once more.

But now it was closer.

Much closer.

"Running only delays the inevitable."

Daniella clutched Russell's jacket, panic twisting her insides.

"What do we do?" she whispered.

Russell looked up into the storm.

Fear.

Love.

Determination.

"All that matters is keeping you alive."

He leaned in, touching his forehead to hers.

His voice was a soft, broken whisper.

"I can't lose you, too."

Daniella's breath shattered.

"I'm not Ashling," she whispered. "I won't disappear. I'm right here."

He kissed her again — softer this time, aching, full of everything he'd been fighting.

Then he pulled back, eyes fierce.

"Run."

She shook her head violently. "No—"

"RUN, DANI."

Another gunshot tore into the concrete inches from her head.

She screamed.

Russell shoved her into the darkness beneath the dam's underpass.

As she stumbled into the shadows, heart ripping apart —

Stryker's silhouette appeared at the top of the stairwell.

Tall.

Still.

Smiling.

"Found you."

And everything went black.

CHAPTER 16 – ASHLING'S GHOST

Darkness swallowed Daniella whole.

The metal grate slammed behind her as she tumbled into the underpass, her palms scraping across cold concrete. Her breath came in sharp, broken bursts; water dripped from the cracks above, echoing like falling glass.

Behind her—

Footsteps.

Slow, steady, deliberate.

Russell's voice roared through the storm.

"RUN, DANI! GO!"

Another gunshot cracked through the night.

She screamed. "RUSSELL!"

Her voice echoed under the dam, swallowed by blackness and the roar of the rushing spillway. Lightning flashed outside, illuminating Stryker's silhouette at the top of the stairwell — tall, calm, a predator hunting in the dark.

Daniella's chest tightened as her world narrowed to one truth:

Russell was hurt.

She felt it like a knife through her ribs.

But she couldn't go back.

If she turned around now, they'd both die.

Her legs moved before her mind caught up, splashing through the run-off stream beneath the dam. Cold water soaked her shoes, her pants, her skin. Every breath burned. Every heartbeat thundered.

A voice carried through the underpass.

Low.

Smooth.

Mocking.

"Daniella..."

She froze.

Stryker's tone was playful, as if they were sharing a private joke.

"You can't hide from me."

She pressed a trembling hand to her mouth.

Her pulse hammered.

She forced herself to keep moving, slipping deeper into the maze beneath the dam — concrete corridors, dripping water, rusted ladders, old maintenance tunnels that smelled of moss and cold steel.

Her camera — the thing that started all this — slammed against her hip with every step.

Ahead, she found a narrow tunnel marked:

MAINTENANCE – AUTHORIZED PERSONNEL ONLY

Perfect.

She pushed through, slamming the iron door shut behind her.

Darkness enveloped her again. Her shaking fingers searched for a light switch.

Nothing.

Only the distant echo of rushing water and—

A groan.

Faint.

Pained.

Male.

Her blood froze.

"Russell?"

Silence.

Then—

Another sound. A low, shaky exhale.

She followed it, stumbling over uneven metal grates as her panic fought her instincts.

She reached the end of the tunnel.

Lightning flashed through a high, broken window, illuminating—

Russell Kane.

Crushed against the wall, one hand clamped over his shoulder, blood seeping between his fingers.

"RUSSELL!"

She ran to him, dropping to her knees. His face was pale, rain-soaked, contorted with pain — but alive.

"Thank God," she sobbed, touching his face. "Thank God—"

He gripped her wrist weakly. "Daniella… go."

"No. I'm not leaving you."

He shook his head, wincing hard. "He's coming. You have to—"

A metallic CLANG tore through the tunnel.

Daniella whipped around.

Stryker had found the maintenance entrance.

His shadow stretched along the wall as he stepped inside.

Russell shoved Daniella toward a second tunnel. "Run. Run now!"

She didn't move.

"I said NO!" she cried, grabbing his face. "I am not leaving you!"

His eyes softened — for a split second.

"You already saved me," he whispered. "Now save yourself."

Footsteps echoed closer.

Three seconds.

Two.

One.

Daniella made a choice.

She grabbed Russell's good arm, slung it around her shoulders, and hauled his weight upward with a strength that came from pure terror.

"No," she whispered fiercely. "We get out of this together."

He stared at her — pain and love and devastation swirling in his eyes.

"You're insane," he breathed.

She shook her head. "I'm yours."

The words hit him like a blow.

And for one heartbeat — even with blood dripping down his arm — he kissed her.

It was fast.

Raw.

Desperate.

Filled with every unspoken word.

Then—

Stryker's voice slid through the dark.

"How touching."

Daniella's heart lurched.

She dragged Russell down the secondary tunnel, slipping on wet metal, stumbling in the dark. Stryker's footsteps followed — slow, confident.

He was playing with them.

Taunting them.

As if he knew the tunnel they were in was a dead end.

Russell's weight grew heavier against her.

"Stay with me," she begged. "Please stay with me."

He gritted his teeth. "Dani—"

"No. Keep going."

They reached a rusted ladder bolted to the wall.

Daniella shoved Russell toward it. "Climb."

He gave a mirthless laugh of pain. "With one arm?"

She set her jaw, placed his foot on the first rung, and pushed upward. "CLIMB!"

He obeyed.

Slowly.

Agonizingly.

Stryker's shadow appeared at the entrance of the tunnel.

"I'm impressed," he said softly. "You're more trouble than Ashling ever was."

Daniella felt rage flare through her fear.

"Go to hell," she snapped.

Stryker smiled in the dark.

"Ladies first."

He raised his gun.

Daniella froze.

But before he could fire—

A metallic WHIR echoed through the tunnel.

Something slid down the ladder shaft above them.

Paper.

Falling like snow.

One landed on Daniella's shoulder.

She grabbed it instinctively.

It wasn't paper at all.

It was a photograph.

Her photograph.

The one she developed—the shot at Rio Dam that caught the silhouette she now knew was Stryker.

But over the image was a handwritten note.

A woman's handwriting.

Elegant. Sharp. Fast.

Daniella recognized it instantly.

Ashling.

LOOK UP.

Daniella snapped her head upward.

A faint glow flickered above — behind the metal grate covering the top of the ladder.

A silhouette leaned over the edge.

A woman's silhouette.

Long hair.

Slim frame.

Wind whipping behind her.

Ashling.

ALIVE.

Daniella gasped.

"ASHLING!"

Russell nearly fell from the ladder. His voice broke. "Ash—?"

But Ashling held up a finger to her lips.

Silence.

Then she bent down — swift, graceful — and used a small metal tool to pry the grate loose.

It fell open with a soft groan.

Stryker's eyes lifted.

"Of course," he murmured. "The traitor returns."

Ashling tossed something down.

A flash drive?

A weapon?

No.

A tiny metal canister.

It hit the ground at Stryker's feet.

A split second later—

BOOM.

A blinding flash.

Smoke exploded through the tunnel.

Stryker hissed, stumbling back.

Daniella screamed.

Russell clung to the ladder.

And Ashling's voice — alive, sharp, commanding — cut through the chaos:

"MOVE, DANI! NOW!"

Daniella didn't think.

Didn't hesitate.

Didn't breathe.

She shoved Russell up the ladder as fast as she could, smoke burning her lungs, adrenaline turning her muscles to steel.

She reached the top, where Ashling's hand shot down and grabbed her wrist.

She pulled Daniella up with surprising strength.

Russell collapsed beside her, bleeding heavily.

Daniella stared at the woman she thought was dead.

Ashling — drenched in rain, dirt-smudged, eyes blazing with something between fury and relief — met her gaze.

"You're late," Ashling said.

Daniella let out a broken laugh. "You're alive."

Ashling smirked. "Unfortunately."

But her eyes softened — disarmingly — as she added,

"I told you I'd protect you."

Daniella's heart twisted.

"You know me," she whispered. "You really know me."

Ashling nodded once.

Then her expression hardened.

"We don't have long. Stryker's not dead."

Russell groaned. Daniella turned to catch him as he collapsed onto her shoulder.

Ashling's face shifted instantly — emotion breaking through her hardened exterior.

She cupped Russell's cheek gently.

"Russell... I'm sorry," she whispered.

His eyes fluttered. "Why...?"

Her voice cracked.

"I never meant to hurt you."

Daniella watched in stunned silence as the truth finally glowed between them like embers.

Ashling loved him.

Not for the mission.

Not for the cover.

Not for the Agency.

But quietly.

Desperately.

Silently.

The way she looked at him now—

the way her hands trembled—

made it undeniable.

Russell whispered, "You left me."

Ashling's tears finally fell.

"I left to save you."

A loud crash echoed from below.

Stryker.

Recovering.

Alive.

Ashling wiped her tears instantly, switching back into operative mode.

"We have to go."

She grabbed Daniella's wrist again.

"And you — you have something he'll kill all of us for."

Daniella swallowed.

"The photograph."

Ashling nodded.

"And something more."

Before Daniella could ask what—

Stryker's voice echoed up the shaft, rougher now, angrier.

"Found you."

Ashling grabbed Russell and Daniella, pulling them into the storm.

"Run," she said.

And this time— they listened.

CHAPTER 17 – THE CONFESSION

Rain hammered the valley.

Cold needles of water sliced through the wind as Ashling pulled Daniella and Russell toward the thick canopy of trees that bordered the dam. The forest swallowed them quickly — wet leaves slapping their faces, mud splashing beneath their feet, branches bowing under the weight of the storm.

Behind them—

A sharp metallic clang echoed

from the ladder shaft

beneath the dam.

Stryker was climbing.

Fast.

"We don't have time," Ashling hissed. Her breath came in short, sharp bursts, but her eyes didn't waver. "Keep moving."

Russell stumbled beside Daniella, leaning heavily onto her shoulder. Blood soaked through the sleeve of his jacket and dripped onto her hand with every step.

"Stop," Daniella begged. "He needs help—"

"No," Ashling cut in. "If we stop, we die. Both of you."

A crack of lightning lit the forest — and for a split second,

Daniella saw Ashling's face clearly.

Pale.

Fierce.

Haunted.

And something else.

Pain.

Ashling wasn't just running.

She wasn't just fighting.

She was breaking.

They pushed deeper into the woods until Ashling suddenly halted at a massive fallen oak, uprooted decades ago, its hollow center forming a natural tunnel.

"Inside," she ordered.

Russell gritted his teeth. "What—are we hiding in a tree?"

"Yes," Ashling barked. "Now."

They crawled into the hollow as the thunder rolled overhead. The inside smelled of damp earth, rot, and old moss. Daniella pressed against Russell, helping him slide down onto his back.

Ashling crouched at the entrance like a guard dog,

scanning the woods with razor-sharp focus.

Only when she was satisfied did she turn back—

—and Daniella saw her face finally crumble.

Ashling's voice softened, cracking at the edges.

"Russell… let me see."

He shook his head weakly. "Don't touch me."

Her breath hitched. "Please."

Slowly—achingly—she reached for him.

He jerked away, wincing. "You lied to me. About everything."

Ashling swallowed hard. Tears gathered but didn't fall.

"Not everything," she whispered.

Russell's voice was raw. "The Agency? The missions? The false name?"

She nodded slowly.

"And Bryan?" he demanded. "He wasn't your brother."

Her gaze lowered. "No."

Russell's voice broke. "He was your partner. Your handler."

Her silence was confirmation enough.

"Why?" Russell whispered, pain twisting through every syllable. "Why did you lie to me? What was I to you?"

Ashling's lips parted — but no sound came out.

Daniella watched her, something twisting in her chest.

Guilt?

No.

Recognition.

Ashling looked like a woman standing in the ruins of something she never meant to break.

Finally — finally — she spoke.

"You were my home."

The words dropped between them like a stone.

Russell froze.

Daniella's breath caught.

Ashling shut her eyes, tears slipping free.

"You were never a cover to me," she said quietly. "Never a mission. Never an assignment. Not to my heart."

Russell's face contorted. "But you left."

"I had to."

"Why?"

Ashling exhaled shakily. "Because Stryker knew."

Russell's jaw tightened. "Knew what?"

Ashling looked at Daniella.

Directly.

Intensely.

With something like reverence.

"That you were the one who saw him."

Daniella's stomach twisted. "Me?"

Ashling nodded.

"You weren't supposed to be on that ridge the night he executed Agent Hale. No civilian was supposed to be anywhere near that location." Her voice lowered. "But you were. With your camera."

Daniella trembled. "I still don't understand—why does that make me a target?"

Ashling moved closer, kneeling in the mud in front of her.

Her eyes softened.

Her voice turned gentle.

Almost protective.

"Because your photograph didn't just show the murder."

She reached out, taking Daniella's hand.

"It showed the reason for it."

Russell frowned. "What reason?"

Ashling swallowed.

"Agent Hale wasn't just a victim. He was a defector. He stole something from the RIO Protocol. Something that Stryker was ordered to retrieve."

Russell leaned forward despite the pain in his shoulder. "Retrieve what?"

Ashling met Daniella's eyes.

"You have it."

The world froze.

Russell stared between them. "She has what?"

Ashling nodded slowly, certainty in every line of her face.

"The thing Hale died for. The thing RIO wants back. The thing Stryker is hunting. The thing the Agency and the rogue operatives and half the damn government want to bury—"

Daniella's voice cracked. "Ashling, what did I do?"

"You took a picture," Ashling whispered. "And you captured

something no one was supposed to see."

Daniella's breath trembled. "What did I capture?"

Ashling leaned closer, her voice slipping into a whisper:

"Hale wasn't alone."

Silence slammed like a door.

"What?" Russell rasped.

Ashling's expression darkened.

"You photographed the person he was meeting."

Daniella clutched her camera instinctively. "But... I didn't see anyone else."

"You didn't," Ashling said. "Not with your eyes."

Daniella blinked. "What does that mean?"

Ashling pointed at her camera.

"You took several shots. One frame captured Stryker. Another captured Hale. But one frame captured—"

A twig snapped outside.

Ashling spun toward the sound, gun raised.

"Quiet," she breathed.

Daniella's heart pounded.

Russell held his breath.

Another snap.

Closer.

Ashling crouched, finger tightening on the trigger.

A shadow moved behind the ferns.

The air went still.

Then—

A small, trembling figure burst into view.

Dirt-streaked.

Soaked.

Mascara smeared.

Breathing hard.

Isla.

Russell's sister-in-law.

Ashling's triplet.

"Oh my God," Daniella whispered. "Isla?"

Isla fell to her knees in the mud.

Her voice cracked.

"He found me."

Ashling's face went white. "Who?"

Isla's entire body shook as she lifted her gaze.

"Stryker."

Lightning flashed.

And in that instant—

Daniella realized Isla wasn't alone.

Behind her—

in the trees—

a silhouette shifted.

Tall.

Still.

Watching.

Stryker.

Ashling swore under her breath.

"We move," she said, grabbing Isla's arm. "Now."

Russell groaned, trying to stand. Daniella clung to him, helping him up.

But Isla collapsed again.

"No," Isla sobbed. "You don't understand."

Ashling froze. "What?"

Isla's voice dropped into a whisper that shattered the world:

"I wasn't running from him."

She lifted a hand — trembling, desperate — pointing at Daniella.

"I was running to her. *"

Daniella's breath stopped.

"Why?" she whispered.

Isla swallowed hard.

Lightning cracked across the sky.

And Isla spoke the words that would change everything:

"Because you're the only one who can save my baby."

Ashling's face drained of blood.

Russell's knees buckled.

Daniella felt the earth tilt beneath her.

"Baby?" she whispered. "Whose baby?"

Isla's tear-filled eyes locked onto Daniella's.

"Hale's," she choked out. "Agent Hale was the father. And Stryker wants the proof."

Daniella's heart slammed against her chest.

Ashling staggered back.

Russell looked sick.

Isla sobbed.

"He wants the evidence Hale carried when he died — the paternity file. And Daniella—"

She pointed at the camera.

"You photographed it."

Daniella felt her world shatter.

And behind Isla—

The silhouette finally stepped into the clearing.

Colin Stryker.

Smiling.

"It's time," he said softly. "Give me the camera, Daniella."

Ashling aimed her gun.

Russell pushed Daniella behind him, trembling.

Isla screamed.

And Stryker spoke the final sentence that turned blood to ice:

"You have ten seconds before I take it from your corpse instead."

CHAPTER 18 – UNDER THE SURFACE

For a heartbeat, the forest didn't move.

No wind.

No birds.

No thunder.

Just the ticking countdown in Daniella's skull.

Ten seconds.

Stryker stood at the edge of the clearing—shadowed, calm, rain sliding down the hard angles of his face like the storm itself bowed around him. His pistol was steady, aimed at Daniella's center mass.

"Camera," he repeated. "Now."

Ashling shifted, moving just half a step in front of Daniella, gun raised, eyes burning.

"You're not touching her," she said.

Stryker's mouth tilted. "Ashling. Always in the way."

Russell swayed where he stood, one arm clamped over his bleeding shoulder, the other held out in front of Daniella like a living shield. His voice came out hoarse, but solid.

"You want the evidence, take it from me," he said. "You've been using me long enough."

Stryker's gaze flicked over him dismissively. "You were never that important, Russell. Just convenient."

Isla sobbed, still on her knees in the mud. "Please, please, please—don't hurt them. I did what you wanted—"

"Not yet," Stryker said. "You led me here. That's all you've done."

Ashling's eyes snapped to Isla. "You led him—?"

Isla shook her head frantically. "He said if I found Daniella, he'd leave the baby out of it. I didn't know he was this close—I didn't know—"

"Lies break my patience," Stryker said mildly. "Enough."

The barrel of his gun lifted that fractional bit higher.

Daniella's fingers dug into the camera strapped cross-body over her chest. It felt heavier now. Knowing what it held made it feel less like a tool and more like a loaded weapon pointed back at all of them.

You took the picture that ruined everything.

Ashling's voice from minutes ago echoed in her head.

You have what Hale died for.

Daniella swallowed hard.

"If I give it to you," she said, forcing her voice to be steady, "you leave them alone. All of them. Russell. Isla. The baby.

Bowman. Ashling."

Ashling hissed. "Daniella, no—"

Stryker smiled.

The expression never reached his eyes.

"Do you honestly think you're in a position to negotiate?"

"I think," Daniella said quietly, "if you shoot me, the camera hits the ground, the card cracks, and your evidence is swimming in the mud." She lifted her chin. "You're not stupid. If you were, you wouldn't scare her this much."

Her head jerked toward Ashling.

Stryker's eyes narrowed.

Thunder rolled over the forest.

"Walk toward me," he said finally. "Slowly. Put the camera on the ground. Then step back."

Russell shook his head. "Daniella—"

She squeezed his fingers once, hard.

"It's okay," she whispered. "I know what I'm doing."

"No, you don't," Ashling snapped. "You're not trained for this—"

"Then stop talking and let me try," Daniella fired back,

surprising herself with the steel in her tone.

Ashling shut her mouth.

Stryker's gun never wavered.

She stepped forward.

Each pace squelched in the mud, rain soaking her jeans, cold water sliding into her boots. Her heart felt too big for her ribs, banging against bone like it needed out.

Seven seconds.

Six.

Five.

She stopped a few feet from him.

Closer than she ever wanted to be.

Up close, she could see the small flecks of silver at his temples, the faint pale scar that ran from his jawline into his collar, the way his eyes—icy, sharp—missed nothing.

No humanity.

Nothing there for her to appeal to.

Just calculation.

"On the ground," he said.

She crouched, the camera strap sliding off her shoulder as

she lowered it to the mud. Her fingers lingered on it for half a breath.

Stryker watched her like a hawk.

Her pulse raced.

This is insane. This is insane. This is—

Her fingertips brushed the small, quick-release latch on the side of the strap. The one she installed after dropping it during a rooftop shoot once. The same quick-release that could send the camera swinging free in an instant.

She clicked it.

The strap dropped like a snake.

She kicked the camera forward.

Stryker's gaze cut down for less than a second.

That was all Ashling needed.

She dove sideways, firing two rapid shots toward his gun hand.

He jerked back, weapon skidding from his grip, a sharp curse ripping from his throat.

"MOVE!" she shouted.

The world exploded into movement.

Russell surged forward despite the pain, grabbing Daniella and yanking her back. Ashling sprinted low, feet sure in the mud as Stryker recovered, lunging toward his fallen weapon.

Isla scrambled sideways, hands over her head, sobbing.

Another flash of lightning.

Another gunshot—

This one not silenced.

It cracked across the clearing like lightning itself.

Stryker spun, shoulder snapping back with the impact.

Bowman.

He stood at the ridge above them, raincoat torn, blood darkening the side of his shirt, gun raised and steady. Somehow, impossibly, he was still on his feet.

"You're harder to kill than I remember," Stryker called up.

"Occupational hazard," Bowman grunted, firing again.

The bullet grazed Stryker's thigh.

Stryker hissed. "Enough."

He dove behind a trunk, hand snatching his gun from the mud as he moved. In a heartbeat, he disappeared into the trees, melting into shadow.

Bowman kept firing until the forest went still.

Then—

Nothing.

Just the rain.

The thunder.

And four ragged people in a clearing, trying not to fall apart.

They didn't speak for a long moment.

The only sounds were Isla's choked sobs, Russell's strained breaths, and the river roaring in the distance like a beast that never slept.

Daniella barely felt the cold.

She turned instantly to Russell, pressing her hands over his wound. His jacket was soaked with blood and rain, the fabric torn at his shoulder.

"Hey," she whispered. "Stay with me, okay?"

He gave her a strained smile. "You keep dragging me back. Hard to leave."

Her throat burned. "Not funny."

"A little funny," he said, then winced.

Ashling was at his other side, expression rigid. "The bullet went clean through. If it hit bone, he'd be screaming louder."

"I can scream louder," he offered weakly.

Ashling ignored him, ripping open a small kit from a pocket inside her jacket—field dressing, gauze, something in a small vial.

She glanced at Daniella. "I need pressure lower. Here."

Daniella obeyed, pressing down where Ashling indicated.

Russell swore under his breath.

"Sorry," she whispered.

He grabbed her wrist with his good hand. "Don't be. I like you, bossy."

Even Ashling's lips twitched for half a heartbeat.

Then the hardness returned.

"You shouldn't have given him the chance to get that close," she snapped at Daniella.

"He already was close," Daniella said quietly. "He was already in my building. At the dam. At my door. I gave you a window."

Ashling held her stare for a long moment.

Then nodded once.

"You did," she conceded. "You bought us time. And you still have the evidence."

Daniella blinked. "No, I—"

She looked down.

Her chest.

Her strap.

Her heart stuttered.

The camera was gone.

"I kicked it right in front of him," she whispered. "It should be—"

She scanned the ground frantically.

The camera lay where Stryker had been standing moments earlier.

The body was missing.

So was the memory card slot cover.

"Shit," Ashling breathed. "He pulled the card."

Panic tightened Daniella's lungs. "Then it's over. He has it. Everything Hale died for. Everything on the SD card—"

Bowman limped down into the clearing, breathing hard. "The SD card from her car is still in my unit," he said. "Back in the city. This was just your camera's card."

"That's bad enough," Ashling muttered. "Now he has part of the puzzle."

Russell tried to sit up straighter, grimacing. "Okay, let's back up. All this talk about 'evidence' and 'proof'—you said she photographed the reason Hale was killed. You said I was her cover. You said Daniella is the only one who can decode this. What does any of that really mean?"

Ashling's shoulders slumped, rain dripping off her lashes.

"The confession," Daniella said softly.

Three heads turned toward her.

She swallowed.

"In the clearing, before Stryker arrived... You said Hale wasn't alone. That I captured the person he was meeting."

Ashling's jaw tightened. "Yes."

"And you said everyone wants to bury that," Bowman added. "Not just Stryker."

"Because it wasn't just some random contact," Ashling said quietly. "It was someone inside the system. Someone high enough that proving it would implode everything they've been running at Rio."

Russell stared at her. "Who?"

Ashling looked at Bowman.

Long.

Heavy.

Loaded.

Bowman's face hardened. "Say it."

She exhaled.

"Agent Hale was meeting his handler's handler," she said. "The one who signed off on every off-book assignment. The one who approved reactivation orders. The one who authorized Stryker's clean-up operations."

She paused.

"The one whose name is all over the RIO Protocol files you just unlocked."

Daniella's hands shook.

"Who?" she whispered.

A beat.

Then Ashling said it.

"Director Michael Bowman."

Silence dropped like an anvil.

Daniella's head snapped toward the detective.

Russell's knuckles whitened on the ground.

Isla stopped sobbing.

Bowman didn't flinch.

His face didn't twist into shock.

Didn't flush with denial.

Didn't even register surprise.

He just closed his eyes, once, like someone finally cut a wire he'd been holding together for years.

"That's not the whole story," he said quietly.

Russell stared at him, voice raw. "You worked for them?"

"I worked against them," Bowman said. "From the inside. You don't expose a corrupt director by filing a complaint. You expose him by letting him think you're one of his own."

Ashling gave a bitter laugh. "You were good at that part."

"I had to be," Bowman said sharply.

Daniella's chest squeezed. "So Hale was meeting—"

"An intermediary," Bowman said. "Someone carrying evidence to prove that I wasn't on their side. They thought I was compromised. That I'd gone soft. That I cared more about the civilians than the program."

"Were they wrong?" Daniella asked.

Bowman's eyes met hers.

"No," he said.

Rain fell harder, like the sky was trying to wash the past away and failing.

"So they sent Stryker to erase Hale," Ashling said. "And to make it look like he was the traitor."

"And you saw it," Bowman added, nodding at Daniella. "Your photograph proves Hale was unarmed. That his hands were up. That someone else was there."

Daniella's throat tightened. "I didn't know."

"You weren't meant to," Ashling replied. "You were supposed to stay a ghost in the background—someone whose work people liked, but whose name never crossed their desks. But then..."

She looked between Daniella and Russell.

"...you came here."

Russell's voice was ragged. "She only came because of me. For the campaign. For the dam. For—"

"You didn't cause this," Ashling cut in sharply. "Stryker caused this. RIO caused this. The Agency caused this. Never forget where the blame belongs."

Isla stirred, voice rough. "Then why is he after me?"

Ashling's hard expression softened as she turned to her sister.

"Because of Hale," she said gently. "Because of the baby. Because if people knew an agent tried to defect with proof— and a living link—that would prove he wasn't a rogue traitor... the story falls apart."

Isla cradled her arms around her stomach.

There was no visible bump yet under her oversized jacket, but Daniella saw the way she curled inward, protective, like she already felt the weight of the life inside her.

"I didn't know who he really was at first," Isla whispered. "He was just... kind. Smart. Sad in this deep way. He told me he wanted out. He wanted to stop doing things that woke him up at night. That he was done being someone's weapon."

Tears spilled down her cheeks.

"He told me he was coming clean," she choked out. "That he had a way to prove everything. That he was meeting someone. I didn't know it would get him killed. I didn't know Stryker—"

Her voice cracked.

"I didn't know I'd be carrying proof inside me."

Ashling's composure fractured.

She moved forward, pulling Isla into a tight embrace.

"You are not proof," Ashling whispered fiercely. "You're my sister. That child is not evidence. He or she is a person. They do not own either of you."

Isla sobbed into her shoulder.

Russell closed his eyes, the pain in his face no longer just physical.

Daniella reached instinctively for his hand.

He took it.

Tightly.

Like it was the only solid grounding left.

"So what now?" Daniella asked quietly.

Bowman exhaled. "Now? We get off this damn ridge before Stryker circles back. He has your card—he'll try to use it to reconstruct what he can. But he doesn't know you still have the original negatives."

She blinked. "The film?"

Bowman nodded. "You shoot digital and film. You've said so."

"I—yes," she said slowly. "For personal work. I processed some. But not all. Some of the dam rolls are still in my darkroom. In my studio."

Ashling's eyes flared. "The studio he's already been inside."

Daniella's stomach dropped. "If he figures that out—"

"He will," Bowman said. "That's why we're going to move before he does."

"How?" Russell asked. "We're bleeding. You're bleeding. We've got a pregnant woman and a photographer who just became a national security threat—"

"International," Ashling corrected. "RIO isn't just domestic anymore."

"Even better," Russell muttered.

Bowman's jaw clenched. "I've got a safe place. Real one this time. Not off a city grid. Somewhere, the usual eyes don't look. We regroup there. Heal. Decide what to do with what you have."

"And if I don't want it?" Daniella asked quietly.

They all looked at her.

"If I destroy it," she continued. "All of it. The negatives. The copies. The SD card. If I walk away—does this stop?"

Ashling's gaze softened.

"If you destroy it," she said gently, "you destroy your leverage. Your proof. And their only reason to keep you alive."

Russell's grip on Daniella's hand tightened painfully.

"No," he said instantly. "We're not giving them that."

She turned to him. "I didn't ask for this."

"I know," he said. "But you're the only one who can finish it."

Her eyes stung.

"That's not fair."

"It's not," he agreed. "None of this is."

He lifted her hand and pressed it briefly to his lips.

"But I will stand next to you every second of it."

Something hot and wild burned behind her ribs.

Fear, Love, Responsibility.

Right or wrong, she wasn't alone anymore.

Ashling straightened, wiping mud and water from her face.

"We don't have time for debate," she said. "We move. Now."

She glanced at Bowman. "You lead. If Stryker has Agency support, he'll have eyes on any official transport."

Bowman nodded once. "I've got my own routes."

He started up the slope toward the tree line, steps slower than usual but still determined.

Russell tried to stand.

His legs nearly gave.

Daniella and Ashling caught him from both sides.

"I've got him," Daniella said, tightening her arm around his waist.

Ashling met her gaze over his shoulder.

Something passed between them.

Respect.

Unease.

Shared ownership of a man caught between them.

"Don't let him fall," Ashling murmured.

"Never," Daniella answered.

Isla pushed herself to her feet, one hand cradling her abdomen.

"Wait," she said suddenly.

They paused.

She looked at Daniella, fear and hope warring in her eyes.

"You said there were photos," she whispered. "Of Hale. Of Stryker. Of his—his murder."

Daniella nodded.

"Yes."

"Then…" Isla swallowed hard. "Does that mean… my baby won't just be a rumor?"

Daniella's chest tightened. "It means he—or she—won't have to grow up in a world where no one believes their father tried to do the right thing."

Isla's lips trembled.

"Then don't destroy it," she said. "Not for me. Not for him."

Daniella nodded.

"Okay."

She felt the weight settle even heavily on her shoulders. But this time, it was different.

This time, it wasn't just about secrets and shadow wars and classified missions.

It was about a child who hadn't even taken their first breath.

About Russell and Ashling and Isla and Bowman and everyone whose lives had been twisted into knots around this dam.

About herself.

The photographer who had gone to capture "quiet"— and accidentally taken a shot loud enough to shake an entire operation.

"Under the surface" wasn't just about the dam.

It was them.

Their guilt.

Their lies.

Their love.

Their choices.

All buried, waiting to rise.

"Let's go," Daniella whispered.

They began the climb.

Behind them, the forest watched silently.

And somewhere deep in the shadows, unseen eyes followed—calculating, waiting, adjusting.

Stryker might have lost this round.

But he had the camera's card.

And he wasn't done.

Not by a long shot.

CHAPTER 19 – SHADOWS IN THE CITY

The forest swallowed them whole.

Rain pelted the canopy above in rhythmic sheets, the storm flattening branches, knocking loose leaves, filling the air with the thick scent of pine and raw earth. The long climb back toward Bowman's hidden route left all five of them soaked, cold, and shivering—but alive.

Barely.

Bowman limped ahead with determination that looked almost inhuman. Blood soaked the left side of his shirt, but he never slowed. He pushed forward like the storm itself was chasing him.

Ashling brought up the rear, her weapon drawn, head swiveling with hypervigilant precision. Every shift of wind, every crack of a twig, every distant roll of thunder made her flinch microscopically—a trained operative reading danger in raindrops.

Daniella stayed at Russell's side, nearly carrying him at moments when his legs weakened. His breathing grew ragged, breath frosting in the cold air.

He leaned more heavily on her the higher they climbed.

"You good?" she whispered.

"No," he admitted. "But you're warm."

She huffed out a breath. "Russell—"

"I'm fine."

He blinked slowly.

"Mostly fine."

A pause.

"Fine-ish."

"You're bleeding," she reminded him.

"Yeah, but you're holding onto me," he murmured. "So that helps."

Her chest tightened painfully.

Behind them, Ashling's voice came sharp:

"He needs rest."

Daniella stiffened.

Ashling moved closer, assessing Russell with a gaze that mixed concern, guilt, and a familiarity Daniella couldn't ignore.

Russell's head tipped back against the tree he was leaning on. "I'm good," he muttered, unconsciously reaching for Daniella's hand again.

Ashling's eyes narrowed—not at him.

At Daniella.

"Keep pressure on his wound," Ashling said coolly.

Her tone was clipped. Professional.

But the tightness around her eyes said more.

Daniella bristled. "I've got him."

Ashling's jaw clenched. "I noticed."

Bowman whirled around, leaning heavily on a fallen log. "If you two are done measuring who's more essential, we need to move."

Silence crackled between Daniella and Ashling.

Russell smirked faintly. "For the record," he murmured, "you're both essential."

"Shut up," the women said at the same time.

Russell snorted, then hissed as pain lanced through his shoulder.

Daniella grabbed his hand. "Okay, enough flirting. Let's go."

Ashling stiffened.

Bowman stepped in. "We're five minutes out."

"Five?" Daniella said hopefully.

Ashling corrected him. "Ten. He says five when he means

ten."

"Fine," Bowman muttered. "Ten."

Russell blinked. "I'm gonna pass out in nine."

"Then pick up your feet in eight," Bowman shot back.

THE SAFEHOUSE

It wasn't a cabin.

Or a building.

Or anything that looked even remotely like shelter.

It was...

A boulder.

Or at least, that's what Daniella thought until Bowman ducked beneath the jutting overhang, felt along a mossy crevice, and pressed something unseen.

A mechanical click echoed, muffled by stone.

A thin seam of light appeared.

The rock face slid aside.

A door.

A hidden concrete bunker built beneath the ridge.

Ashling exhaled in a whisper. "I thought this place was just a rumor."

Bowman grunted. "Good. Means it stayed a secret."

Inside was dim, cold, and metallic—an underground fallout shelter retrofitted with a cot, old military crates, a rusted sink, lanterns, and stacks of canned supplies. No windows. One single ventilation shaft. It smelled faintly of old oil and dust.

Russell collapsed onto the cot with a groan.

Daniella knelt beside him instantly.

Ashling hovered a foot away, pacing, arms crossed, jaw clenched tight.

Bowman sealed the door behind them with a heavy metal bar.

The silence that followed was absolute.

Just their breaths.

And the distant roar of the storm filtered through the concrete.

Daniella peeled Russell's jacket down gently. "Tell me if this hurts."

"It all hurts," he murmured, "but your hands are soft, so that helps."

Her heart gave a painful kick.

Ashling turned away sharply.

Bowman rummaged through an old crate. "Here. Field suture kit."

Russell groaned. "Ashling, don't let her near me with a needle. She'll stab me out of spite."

Ashling glared at him. "I don't stab people I care about."

Daniella froze.

Ashling froze.

Russell blinked slowly. "You... what?"

She looked away instantly. "Just shut up and let her stitch you."

But the words hung between them—heavy, unsaid, too late to take back.

Daniella's stomach twisted.

He cared for Ashling.

Once.

Maybe still.

But now he was looking at Daniella.

Only Daniella.

His eyes softened.

"Hey," he murmured. "Eyes up here."

She snapped back to the present.

"Right," she said. "Sorry. Medical crisis. Needle. Blood. Focus."

He smiled softly. "You're cute when you panic."

She stabbed the needle into his skin.

He yelped.

Ashling snorted. "Deserved."

When he was bandaged, Russell fell asleep instantly—exhaustion dragging him under.

Daniella sat on the ground beside him, back pressed to the concrete wall, knees curled to her chest. Her fingers traced the strap of the camera she'd salvaged from the mud—even without the card, it felt like a living thing.

A piece of herself.

Ashling watched her from across the room.

Finally, she spoke:

"You're changing everything."

Daniella looked up. "What?"

"You were supposed to be a footnote."

Ashling's voice was quiet. "A photographer. A civilian. Not a variable."

"Sorry," Daniella whispered, "for existing, I guess."

Ashling didn't smile.

"You don't understand," she murmured. "Russell… wasn't supposed to love anyone after me."

Daniella's heart clenched painfully.

"He doesn't—" she started.

Ashling cut her off with a glare.

Sharp.

Painful.

Familiar.

"Don't lie," Ashling said. "Not to me. Not when he looks at you like that."

Daniella looked away.

"And," Ashling added quietly, "you look back the same."

Daniella swallowed hard. "This isn't the time—"

"You're right," Ashling said. "It's not."

They sat in thick silence.

Isla finally stirred from her corner of the safehouse,

whispering:

"You both should stop."

The sisters turned toward her.

Isla hugged her knees protectively. "We're fighting for our lives. For my baby's life. Not for some man. He's great, yes. Cute, yes. But he's not the universe."

Daniella flushed.

Ashling's eyes softened.

Isla continued. "Let him choose his own heart. But don't let it tear yours apart in the process."

Her voice cracked.

"Because the real enemy is out there."

Daniella nodded.

Ashling nodded.

Something unspoken settled between them.

A truce.

Temporary or not, it was enough.

BOWMAN'S WARNING

When Russell finally woke hours later, pale but stable, the bunker felt strangely calm.

Until Bowman spoke.

"We'll be leaving at dawn," he said. "Into the city."

Daniella frowned. "New York? Why?"

Bowman turned toward her, expression grave.

"Because Stryker has already contaminated the Rio Dam. He's reported a fabricated story to local authorities. He's setting the stage to pin everything—including Hale's death—on you."

Daniella's stomach dropped. "Me?"

"Not officially," Bowman said. "Not yet. But soon. He already has his narrative forming. And worse—he's using the stolen memory card to back it up."

Russell sat upright, wincing. "Using it how?"

Bowman ran a hand through his hair.

"He's manipulating the photos. Making it look like Daniella was there with Hale. Making it look like she took money from him. Making it look like she lured him to the dam."

Ashling cursed under her breath. "He's building a case."

"A fake case," Bowman said. "One the Agency will accept.

Because they want this tied up with a bow."

Daniella's chest tightened. "So if we don't stop him…"

"You'll be hunted," Bowman said. "By law enforcement. By the Agency. By the press. By anyone looking for a scapegoat."

Russell grabbed her hand.

She looked at him.

He looked at her.

And the world narrowed.

"We do this together," he said quietly. "All of it."

Her throat burned. "What if I'm not built for this?"

"You are," he whispered. "You just don't know it yet."

Ashling muttered something under her breath, but the jealousy was softer this time. Almost sad.

"Dawn," Bowman repeated. "We head to the city. We confront the Director himself. And we expose everything."

Daniella's pulse pounded.

The city.

The Agency.

The evidence.

Her film.

Her name.

Her life.

"All of it ends there," Bowman said.

"No," Ashling corrected, her voice low and fierce.

"All of it begins there."

Thunder cracked outside.

Stryker was somewhere in the trees.

Waiting.

Hunting.

And tomorrow—

Daniella would walk right into the heart of the storm.

CHAPTER 20 – THE HIDDEN THREAD

Dawn never really came.

The storm simply... thinned.

The sky over the Hudson shifted from pitch-black to a washed-out charcoal, clouds hanging low and heavy over the valley like they were too tired to move. The rain didn't stop, but it softened to a fine mist that clung to skin, hair, and clothing.

Inside the bunker, it was hard to tell what time it was at all.

Only Bowman's watch said 5:17 a.m.

He snapped the metal bar off the door and shouldered it open.

"Time's up," he said. "We move."

Russell stirred on the cot, face pale but eyes clearer than the night before. Daniella's jacket had been folded beneath his head as a makeshift pillow. She hadn't slept; her body hummed with a jittery exhaustion that felt worse than being fully tired.

She pushed herself upright as Bowman held the door.

Cold air rushed in.

Wet.

Sharp.

Real.

"You good?" she asked Russell.

He smirked weakly. "Define good."

"You're upright and breathing," Ashling said. "That's good enough."

He swung his legs over the side of the cot with a hiss. "Didn't know sarcasm was part of the Agency's official toolkit."

"It's in the fine print," Ashling said. But the corner of her mouth twitched.

Isla rose more slowly, one hand on the wall, the other at her stomach. She looked even smaller in the bunker light—a young woman caught in a war she never signed up for.

"You okay?" Daniella asked her.

"No," Isla said honestly. "But I'm coming anyway."

Daniella nodded. "Okay. Then we're okay."

They hiked back along a narrow, hidden trail that wound down the opposite side of the ridge from the dam. The trees rustled quietly, dripping with last night's rain. The world looked scrubbed raw—sharp edges, muted colors, everything still in that strange, breathless hush after a storm.

Bowman led them to a gravel service road where an old dark-blue SUV waited under the skeletal remains of a rusted radio tower.

"This thing gonna make it?" Russell asked.

"It's got more lives than I do," Bowman said, tossing him a tired look. "In."

They piled in—Bowman driving, Ashling in the passenger seat, the others in the back. Russell took the middle spot; Daniella pressed against his right side, careful of his shoulder, and Isla against the other.

As the SUV rattled to life and started for the highway, the world outside blurred into trees and stone and the occasional glimpse of water through the fog.

"Where exactly are we going?" Daniella asked.

"First stop?" Bowman said. "Your studio."

Her stomach clenched. "He's been there."

"Probably," Bowman said. "But if your film is still there, we need it. If it's gone, we need to know that too."

Ashling twisted in her seat to look at Daniella. "How many rolls from Rio Dam didn't you process?"

"Three," Daniella said. "One I developed. Two are still in canisters, labeled. They're in a container on the second shelf in the darkroom."

"Any backup?" Ashling asked.

"Digital scans of the ones I processed," she said. "On an external drive. Unplugged. That's all."

Bowman nodded. "Then we grab the canisters and the drive, and we go dark again."

"And then?" Russell asked.

"And then," Bowman said, "we see what else you caught that none of us realized."

The city rose out of the gray morning like a mirage—buildings shrouded in low clouds, windows reflecting the dull light, traffic already snarling despite the hour. Manhattan looked the same as it always did from a distance—

But for Daniella, it didn't feel the same anymore.

Her city.

Her streets.

Her skyline.

And somewhere inside it, people were being handed a lie with her name on it.

She watched the buildings approach through the fogged passenger window, heart pounding.

"Breathe," Russell murmured beside her, his good hand folding over hers.

"I am," she said. "I just forgot how."

He gave her a small smile. "I'll remind you."

Ashling noticed. Of course she did.

Her grip tightened on the dashboard.

Bowman took a series of back roads off the main highway, avoiding toll cameras and major intersections. He weaved through older industrial blocks and quieter side streets until he finally pulled into an underground parking garage beneath a nondescript brick building in SoHo.

Daniella knew this building.

Her building.

Her throat went tight.

"Okay," Bowman said. "We go in fast. If anything looks off, we walk away. We don't engage. We don't improvise. We don't try to be heroes."

"Too late," Russell said under his breath.

Bowman ignored him.

They stepped out into the dim, concrete chill of the garage.

It was quiet.

Too quiet.

No other cars on that level. No footsteps. No security guard. Just the low hum of the city above and a flickering fluorescent light over the stairwell door.

Daniella's heart climbed into her throat as they climbed to the third floor.

Her floor.

The hallway looked normal.

Same scuffed baseboards. Same peeling exit sign. Same faint smell of paint and coffee, and someone's leftover curry from the night before.

Her studio door, halfway down the corridor, stood closed.

No broken lock.

No splintered frame.

No caution tape.

Just closed.

Ashling stepped ahead, checking the angles, her body relaxed but ready. Bowman kept one hand near his concealed weapon.

Daniella's fingers shook as she reached into her pocket for the key.

"Let me," Bowman said quietly.

She handed it over.

He slid the key into the lock—

And paused.

"What?" Russell whispered.

Bowman listened for a breath.

Then turned the knob.

The door opened.

No flash.

No immediate movement.

Just the familiar smell of her life.

Coffee.

Chemical fix.

Paper.

City air through cracked windows.

It looked...Exactly the same.

Daniella stepped inside on shaky legs.

Her photos still lined the wall—portraits, cityscapes, a collection of Rio Dam test prints pegged to a line.

The desk was as she'd left it.

The couch was still messy with blankets.

The darkroom door was closed.

"No sign of forced entry," Ashling said, scanning the space. She opened drawers quickly, eyes sharp. "Mess level consistent with artist. Could be staged, but it feels natural."

"Yeah," Russell said, managing a small crooked smile. "Feels like her."

Daniella moved straight to the darkroom.

She hesitated.

Then pushed the door open.

The red safelight glowed dimly overhead.

Tanks.

Trays.

Clips.

Shelves.

Her labeled film canister container sat where she'd left it on the second shelf to the right.

Exactly where it should be.

She grabbed it with trembling fingers.

Three canisters inside.

All three labeled.

RIO – A

RIO – B

RIO – C

She exhaled a shaky breath.

"They're here."

Bowman stepped into the doorway. "Good. Grab them and the external drive. Then we're gone."

"On it," she said.

She crossed the small room to the metal cabinet where she kept her tech backups. The external drive sat tucked behind a box of old contact prints.

She froze.

There was a yellow sticky note on top of it.

Her name in block letters.

D –

Her stomach dropped.

Her fingers shook as she peeled it up and read the neat, precise handwriting.

You take beautiful pictures.

I like the ones where you don't realize someone is behind you.

— C.S.

Her vision tunneled.

"Ashling," she whispered.

Ashling appeared in the doorway instantly. "What is it?"

Daniella handed her the note.

Ashling's jaw locked.

"He's been here," she said. "He didn't take the film because he wanted you to know he could have."

She crushed the note in her fist.

Bowman's expression darkened. "We've stayed too long."

Daniella stuffed the canisters and drive into her bag, hand brushing her camera case out of reflex.

They moved for the door.

On the way out, Daniella's gaze snagged on the Rio Dam test prints on the line.

One in particular.

A wide shot of the water and rocks and spillway. Once, it had just been a study in light and shadow.

Now—

Ashling's voice echoed: You photographed the person he was meeting.

Daniella stepped closer.

"What are you doing?" Russell whispered.

"Wait," she murmured.

She studied the print. It was small—eight by ten—grainy from the distance.

But in the far corner of the frame, near the blurred edge of the spillway, a darker smudge stood against the concrete.

A figure.

Half-hidden.

Facing away.

You didn't see it with your eyes.

But the camera did.

She pulled the print off the line.

"Bring it," Bowman said. "We'll blow it up later."

"No," she said quietly. "We can do it now."

They didn't leave the building.

Not yet.

Bowman hustled them up one more flight of stairs to the empty office space above—once an architecture firm, now a dusty storage floor with abandoned drafting tables and flickering lights.

"This place isn't on my lease," he said. "It's a sublet no one maintained. No cameras. No utilities in use. It's invisible on the books."

"Comforting," Russell muttered.

Bowman cleared off a table near the window and set up Daniella's laptop, external drive, and a portable scanner from his bag.

"You carry that around?" Russell asked.

"Never leave home without it," Bowman said.

They scanned the print at the highest resolution the old machine allowed. The file appeared on screen—grainy, gray, filled with fog and stone and water.

"There," Daniella said, pointing. "Bottom right."

Bowman zoomed.

The smudge became a blur.

The blur became a shape.

The shape became a person.

Still grainy.

But more defined now.

A man in a dark coat.

Standing near Hale.

Head turned away.

"Can you sharpen it?" Ashling asked.

Bowman ran a series of low-level enhancements—adjusting contrast, clarity, pulling detail out of shadow.

The pixels tightened.

A jawline emerged.

A collar.

The faint suggestion of a tie.

And on the wrist—

A watch.

Daniella leaned closer.

Ashling sucked in a breath.

"No," she said.

Russell frowned. "What? What is it?"

Bowman didn't speak.

He didn't have to.

On the screen was a face they all recognized from news clips, internal memos, and the RIO file header.

Director James Mercer.

The man technically above Bowman.

The one who signed the approvals.

The one the Agency trusted.

He had been at the dam the night Hale died.

In person.

"Holy shit," Russell whispered.

Ashling exhaled, everything clicking into place. "That's why they need the photos gone. Why Stryker's desperate. Why RIO is scrambling. They can explain away a rogue handler. They can't explain away the Director being on-site at an execution."

Isla's voice trembled. "He was there when Hale died?"

"Yes," Bowman said, jaw clenched. "And now we have proof. Real proof. Not just whispers."

Daniella stared at the image.

She hadn't meant to capture this.

She'd just liked the way the light fell.

Her throat burned.

"I didn't ask for this," she whispered.

"No," Bowman agreed. "But you're the only one who has it."

The laptop chimed.

A notification popped up in the corner of the screen.

No one had touched anything.

No one had opened a browser.

But the Wi-November 14, 2025yes had auto-connected to the building's network.

And now—

A news site headline slid onto the screen with a breaking banner.

HUDSON VALLEY PHOTOGRAPHER PERSON OF INTEREST IN FEDERAL CASE

Below the headline—

A photo of her.

One taken from her own website.

Daniella froze.

"Click it," Ashling said.

Bowman opened the link.

The article loaded—already circulated, already embedded with three still images taken from her stolen memory card.

Image 1: Daniella near the dam.

Image 2: Daniella's silhouette on the ridge.

Image 3: Hale, blurred—standing too close to her, the manipulation making it look like they were meeting.

"Son of a—" Bowman hissed. "He moved fast."

The article text blurred in Daniella's vision.

"... federal authorities seeking to question New York–based photographer Daniella Russo in connection with an ongoing investigation..."

"... believed to be the last civilian with access to the missing federal consultant..."

"... sources report potential ties to leaked imagery..."

Her name.

Her face.

Her work.

Twisted.

Russell's hand found hers under the table. "We'll fix it," he said.

Her voice cracked. "How?"

"By staying ahead of him," Bowman said. "This leak means Stryker jumped the gun. The Agency will be scrambling for a narrative. That gives us a window."

Ashling nodded slowly. "He just made her visible. We make the truth louder than his lie."

Isla leaned against the wall, one hand clutching her jacket closed. "And if you don't?"

"Then they bury all of us," Bowman said.

Silence settled.

Not the helpless silence of before.

The kind of silence that comes when everyone realizes there's no off-ramp left.

Only one road forward.

"What's the plan?" Daniella asked.

Bowman's gaze dropped to the image of Director Mercer on the screen.

"The hidden thread in this entire operation has always

been him," Bowman said. "Not Hale. Not Stryker. Not even Ashling. Everything runs through Mercer."

"And now," Ashling added, nodding at the zoomed-in frame, "you've tied him to the scene of a murder."

Bowman's mouth hardened.

"We leak it," he said. "But not to them. Not to any outlet they can influence. We take it to someone they can't control."

"Who's that?" Russell asked.

Bowman's lips twitched.

"A woman who hates the Agency more than I do."

Ashling's eyebrows rose. "You're talking about Rivera?"

"Yeah."

"Isn't she the one who called you a 'corrupt relic' on national television?" Ashling asked.

"Yes," Bowman said, a little too calmly. "Which is why she'll listen when I tell her where the bodies are buried."

Daniella blinked. "Who is she?"

"Investigative journalist," Ashling said. "Former embedded reporter. Got burned when she tried to expose a black site in Eastern Europe and the Agency gaslit her into oblivion."

"She has reach," Bowman said. "She has rage. She has

nothing left to lose. And she's been waiting for something like this."

He looked at Daniella.

"Someone like you."

Her heart stuttered. "Me?"

"You're the one who took the picture," he said. "You're the one they're trying to frame. You're the one with the moral authority in this story. People will believe you before they believe me."

"Or me," Ashling said softly.

Daniella looked from the screen to Russell, to Isla, to Ashling, to Bowman.

The hidden thread.

Mercer.

Stryker.

RIO.

The dam.

Hale.

The baby.

Her.

It's all connected.

Because of the light on water.

Because she clicked the shutter.

Fear pressed against her ribs like a physical weight.

"I don't know how to do this," she whispered.

Russell squeezed her hand.

"You already did," he said quietly. "The day you raised the camera."

Ashling nodded once. "Now you just have to decide what kind of story you want that picture to tell."

Bowman closed the laptop with a quiet click.

"Pack it up," he said. "We're going to meet Rivera."

"And where is she?" Russell asked.

Bowman's answer was simple.

"Exactly where everyone does their best work," he said.

"In the shadows."

CHAPTER 21 – A DANGEROUS ATTRACTION

Manhattan swallowed them whole.

The city was already stretching awake — yellow cabs slicing through early traffic, steam rising from the grates, coffees gripped in hurried hands. To everyone else, it was just another morning.

To Daniella, it felt like stepping onto a battlefield.

Bowman kept his head down as he led them through the maze of side streets toward the Lower East Side. Isla's hood was pulled low, her steps careful. Ashling's hand hovered near her jacket zipper, where a weapon was hidden. Russell stayed close, his shoulder brushing Daniella's with every breath.

"You're sure Rivera will come alone?" Russell asked.

"No," Bowman said. "But her people aren't Agency. They don't salute Mercer."

"Comforting," Isla murmured.

Daniella tried to swallow the rising panic, but it clung to her throat like smoke.

The article about her had already spread.

People were sharing it on buses.

Phones lit up on the subway platforms.

Screens over bodegas flashed her face.

Everywhere she looked, it felt like eyes lingered too long.

Russell noticed.

He slid his hand around her waist, drawing her closer as they crossed the street. His presence was warm, steady, grounding.

"You're not alone," he said quietly.

"I know," she whispered. But fear still trembled beneath her ribs.

Ashling noticed too. She stopped walking, just for a moment, eyes locking onto Russell's hand on Daniella's hip.

A storm briefly passed through her expression.

Sharp.

Jealous.

Heartbroken.

Daniella felt it.

Russell missed it.

Bowman ignored it.

"We're here," he said finally.

RIVERA

The meeting point was a narrow alley behind an old brick print shop. Graffiti covered the walls in layered murals and faded tags. A metal door sat at the far end, no signs, no markings.

Bowman knocked twice.

Paused.

Then three more times.

A sliding metal panel opened.

Two sharp brown eyes stared out.

"Password?" the voice asked.

Bowman exhaled. "I hate this part. Just let us in, Rivera."

A soft, amused scoff.

The door opened.

Standing there was a woman in her early fifties — short black hair streaked with silver, leather jacket, boots that had seen war zones, and a gaze that instantly dissected every threat in front of her.

"Michael Bowman," she said, voice smooth but cutting. "You always bring me the most interesting problems."

"Wish I didn't," Bowman said. "But here we are."

Rivera stepped aside.

"Come in. Quickly."

Inside was a dimly lit room filled with printers, screens, abandoned desks, old newspaper clippings, coffee mugs, half-soldered electronics, and enough conspiracy corkboards to make a detective jealous.

Ashling scanned the corners, noting exits, vents, and shadows.

Russell helped Isla into a chair.

Rivera's gaze landed on Daniella.

"You," she said. "The photographer."

Daniella stiffened. "Yes."

Rivera nodded slowly. "I saw the article. They're sloppy. They're rushing. That means what you have is dangerous enough to scare them."

She turned to Bowman. "Show me."

Bowman opened the laptop and pulled up the enhanced scan of the photograph — Director Mercer at the dam.

Rivera froze mid-step.

"Well," she whispered. "I'll be damned."

Russell leaned forward. "You believe it?"

"Believe it?" Rivera laughed humorlessly. "Sweetheart, I've been calling Mercer a snake for years. This just gives me a fangs-on-camera closeup."

Ashling folded her arms. "We need it out there."

"No," Rivera said. "Not yet."

Daniella frowned. "Why not?"

Rivera pointed at her.

"Because if I publish this now, you disappear. Permanently. Mercer's people will come for you before the ink dries on the headline."

The room fell still.

Rivera walked up to Daniella, close enough that Daniella could smell cigarettes and peppermint on her breath.

"You didn't just take a lucky picture. You stepped into a war most people don't know exists."

Daniella's voice was soft. "I didn't mean to."

"Doesn't matter," Rivera said. "You're in it now."

Russell stepped between them protectively. "What's our play?"

Rivera walked to a cluttered desk, pulled out a worn notebook, and flipped it open.

"You need to give me everything," she said. "The original negatives, the undeveloped film, and a statement from you."

"No," Ashling snapped instantly.

Everyone looked at her.

Ashling shook her head. "She sends that film to Rivera, and Mercer knows exactly who to eliminate first. Daniella isn't trained for this. She isn't insulated. She's exposed."

"Then insulate her," Rivera said. "Unless your jealousy's clouding your judgment."

The temperature in the room dropped.

Ashling stepped forward, eyes going hard. "Watch your mouth."

Rivera smirked. "Touched a nerve, did I? Your type always does—deadly in the field, useless in love."

Daniella's breath caught.

Ashling's fists clenched.

"Enough," Bowman barked.

But the damage was done.

Russell took Daniella's hand.

Ashling saw it.

Her face fell—just for a heartbeat—before she masked it behind steel.

Daniella felt the weight of Ashling's pain settle into the room like an invisible fog.

She didn't know how to fix it.

She didn't know if she should.

Rivera tapped her notebook sharply. "If the girl doesn't testify, the evidence is nothing. Mercer will call this doctored. Fabrication. Deepfake. Whatever fits the story. He'll bury it."

Daniella swallowed hard. "So… what are you saying?"

Rivera's gaze pierced her.

"You need to be the face of this," she said. "You need to speak before Mercer paints you as a criminal. You need to go public first."

Bowman stiffened. "Rivera—"

"She's right," Isla whispered suddenly.

Everyone turned.

Isla looked fragile, trembling, but her voice held surprising strength.

"You're the only one they can't discredit," she said quietly. "He already tried to frame you. You beat him to his own lie by telling your truth."

Daniella stared at her.

"I can't," she whispered. "I don't want to be a hero. I take pictures. I don't—"

Russell pulled her aside, away from the others.

Into the corner of the room.

Just the two of them.

His fingers slid along her jaw.

His forehead touched hers.

"Listen to me," he said softly. "You're stronger than you know."

Her breath trembled. "Russell—"

"I believe in you."

His voice dropped lower.

Softer.

More intimate.

"You saved me at that dam. You saved Isla without even knowing. And you took the picture that can take down the man who killed Hale."

Her eyes burned. "I'm scared."

"So am I," he whispered. "But I'm with you. Every step."

His thumb brushed her cheek.

She leaned into him before she could stop herself.

Ashling watched from across the room, eyes darkening, chest rising and falling with uneven breaths.

Rivera noticed.

Of course she did.

The air thrummed.

Russell's voice was a breath against her lips:

"You don't have to be fearless. Just be you."

Daniella closed her eyes.

For one brief, aching second— she let herself feel it.

All of it.

The warmth.

The pull.

The promise.

Then—

The window shattered.

A bullet exploded through the glass, embedding in the plaster inches above Ashling's head.

"DOWN!" Bowman roared.

Rivera dropped behind a desk.

Isla screamed and covered her stomach.

Ashling lunged for her gun.

Russell slammed Daniella to the floor, shielding her with his body.

More shots burst through the window in rapid succession.

Glass rained down.

Concrete splintered.

Lights flickered.

Bowman crawled to the wall, peering out through the broken frame.

"Sniper!" he shouted. "East rooftop!"

Ashling fired back blindly, bullets ripping into brick across the alley.

"Who is it?" Russell yelled.

Bowman gritted his teeth.

His face went dark.

"Stryker," he said. "He found us."

Rivera cursed. "We need to get out. Now."

Bowman pointed to a metal grate on the floor. "Basement access. Old sewer line. MOVE!"

Daniella scrambled after him as more bullets tore through the room. Ashling grabbed Isla, dragging her behind a toppled cabinet. Russell covered Daniella with his uninjured arm, guiding her to the grate.

Bowman ripped it open.

A black tunnel yawned below.

Rivera jumped first.

Then Isla.

Then Ashling.

Daniella hesitated.

Russell put a hand on her cheek.

"I won't let anything happen to you," he said.

Then he kissed her.

Desperate.

Brief.

Like a promise stamped in fire.

"Go," he whispered.

She jumped.

Russell followed, pulling the grate shut just as another bullet hit the floor where his head had been a second earlier.

The tunnel below was dark.

Wet.

Echoing.

Claustrophobic.

Ashling took the lead, flashlight cutting through the shadows.

Bowman whispered back:

"Everyone, move. Quietly. Stay low."

Behind them— faint, distant— footsteps echoed through the alley above.

Stryker wasn't done.

He was hunting.

And the deeper they went into the belly of the city, the clearer one truth became—

This wasn't just a conspiracy anymore.

It was a war.

And Daniella was the flashpoint.

CHAPTER 22 – DOUBLE EXPOSURE

The tunnel swallowed their voices.

Water dripped from somewhere up ahead in slow, hollow plinks. The air was damp and cold, smelling faintly of mildew, rust, and old secrets. Their footsteps echoed along the narrow brick corridor, the sound bouncing back at them like a second set of ghosts following behind.

Ashling led, flashlight cutting a narrow beam through the darkness. Rivera moved just behind her, muttering coordinates under her breath. Bowman brought up the rear, one hand near his sidearm, the other trailing the wall to feel for turns.

In the middle, Daniella kept pace with Russell and Isla.

Russell's arm brushed her shoulder with every step, his uninjured hand hooked loosely in her bag strap like he was anchoring himself there. His breathing was quick, a little too shallow. Each time his boots slipped on the slick ground, her heart leapt.

"You still with me?" she whispered.

"Mostly," he murmured. "Tunnel's spinning, though. Tell it to stop."

"That's the concussion and blood loss," Isla said quietly. "Very scientific assessment."

Russell huffed out a breath. "You sound like my sister."

"That's because she loved you," Isla said.

He fell silent.

Daniella squeezed his fingers in the dark.

They turned left, then right, then followed a gentle downward slope. The walls shifted from old brick to rough concrete, tagged with graffiti from some long-gone city crew.

"Where does this go?" Daniella asked.

"Abandoned service lines," Rivera said. "Back when this neighborhood still had a different name and a different kind of crime."

"So… not safer crime," Russell said.

"Just less formalized," Rivera replied.

Ashling stopped at a junction where three tunnels met.

Her flashlight beam swept over each one.

Right: more darkness, faint hum of distant pipes.

Left: trickle of water and the scent of sewage.

Straight: silence.

She closed her eyes, listening.

Bowman's voice came low. "What do you hear?"

"Nothing," she said.

"Good nothing or bad nothing?"

She tilted her head.

"Bad," she decided. "It's too clean."

Daniella frowned. "Clean?"

Ashling turned to them.

"If Stryker knew Rivera's meeting spot, he knew her escape routes," she said. "He was aiming to pin us there. The tunnels are obvious. If I were him, I'd be waiting at the end of at least one."

Bowman squinted into the darkness. "You think he's ahead of us?"

"He's always ahead of us," Ashling said. "We're just catching up slowly."

Isla's voice trembled. "So what do we do?"

Rivera pointed down the right tunnel. "That one feeds into a maintenance shaft beneath an old subway line. From there, we can surface into a storage room two blocks east of here. Not many people know it exists."

"I know it exists," Ashling said. "Which means Stryker might, too."

"We don't have better," Bowman said.

Daniella's phone buzzed.

The sound sliced through the tunnel.

Everyone froze.

Her mind raced. Who even still has my number?

She pulled it out slowly, shielding the screen with her hand to avoid flooding the tunnel with light.

UNKNOWN NUMBER

Subject line:

YOU MISSED A SPOT.

Attached:

A single image.

Her own face.

Shot from above.

In Rivera's office.

It was taken seconds before the first bullet shattered the window.

The angle was wrong for a sniper scope.

It came from inside.

Daniella's breath stuttered. "Oh my God..."

Russell leaned closer. "What is it?"

She turned the screen slightly so only he and Ashling could see.

Ashling's jaw clenched.

Stryker's answer arrived as a text beneath the image:

You keep looking out the window.

You should worry more about who stands behind you.

A chill rippled down Daniella's spine.

"Rivera," Ashling said sharply. "Who else knew you were meeting us?"

The journalist shrugged. "No one. I don't send calendar invites, Agent Moore."

"Your own people?" Bowman pressed. "Any of them could've passed word along."

Rivera set her jaw. "If I thought my team was talking to Mercer's people, I'd have buried them myself."

Another drip echoed somewhere ahead.

Daniella stared at the phone.

This wasn't just surveillance.

This was...

Double exposure.

Two realities at once: the one she remembered, and the one he was manufacturing around it. Her life being overlaid with another version until even she started to question which was true.

She shoved the phone back into her pocket.

"I'm done letting him direct the narrative," she whispered.

Ashling studied her for a long moment.

Then nodded once.

"That's the right rage," she said. "Hold onto it."

They chose the right tunnel.

The air grew colder as they walked, the sound of distant trains faintly rumbling above them. Water dripped more steadily now, forming shallow pools that caught and distorted the flashlight beam.

Russell stumbled.

Daniella caught him, his weight heavy against her.

"You okay?" she murmured.

"Define okay," he tried again.

"That joke is expired," she said. "Try another."

"Okay," he said weakly. "I... really want to kiss you right now."

She almost dropped him.

"Russell," she hissed, feeling heat rise to her face despite the cold. "You are bleeding and possibly concussed."

"Yeah," he said. "That's probably why I said it out loud."

Ashling glanced back, jaw tightening.

Daniella's heart twisted.

She lowered her voice. "We'll talk about it when you're not leaking."

"Romantic," he chuckled, winced, and leaned more heavily on her. "But I'll take it."

The maintenance ladder appeared at last, bolted to one wall where the tunnel widened into a concrete pit.

Ashling swept the light up.

"Fifteen feet," she said. "Hatch at the top. Could be locked."

Bowman stepped forward. "I'll go first."

Rivera snorted. "You're bleeding."

"So is everyone," he said. "I'm heavier. If the ladder's going to break, I'd rather it break under me."

He started to climb.

The metal creaked but held.

Halfway up, Daniella heard it—

A faint hiss.

Soft.

Persistent.

Wrong.

"Ashling," she whispered. "Do you hear that?"

Ashling lifted the light.

Her gaze snapped to a small vent halfway up the wall, near the corner.

A thin stream of vapor leaked from it, curling across the ladder in a barely visible plume.

She didn't hesitate.

"EVERYONE DOWN!" she shouted. "NOW!"

Bowman dropped from the ladder, landing hard, grunting as his knees hit concrete. Rivera stumbled back. Isla clutched her jacket tighter.

"What is it?" Russell asked.

Ashling's voice went flat.

"Gas."

Daniella's blood ran cold.

"Poison?" she choked.

Ashling inhaled cautiously, nostrils flaring.

"No smell," she said. "Fast-acting sedative, most likely. That's his style. Put us to sleep, drag out who he needs, leave the rest."

"So he can separate us," Bowman said. "Pick us off."

"Ashling, can we go back?" Rivera asked.

Ashling shook her head. "If he rigged this vent, he's probably rigged others. He wants to flush us into his net."

Daniella's heart raced.

They were trapped between a gas-filled climb and a potentially compromised backtrack.

Classic funnel.

Double exposure again—two bad choices at once.

"Options," Russell said. "We need options."

Ashling paced, light swinging. "These old tunnels usually have branch drains somewhere lower. Overflow channels. If we can find one, it might lead us to a lower grate or another access point."

"So we go down," Isla said softly. "Not up."

Bowman grimaced. "Down into what?"

Ashling met his gaze.

"The part of the city no one wants to remember exists," she said. "Old infrastructure. Forgotten chambers. Places people like Mercer built things they didn't want people to see."

"Like black sites," Rivera muttered.

"Like black sites," Ashling agreed.

Daniella swallowed.

"And if there isn't another outlet?" she asked.

"Then we've already suffocated," Ashling said. "So it won't matter."

**

They followed the sound of water.

Not the gentle drip they'd heard before.

A louder rush.

Like a river trapped in stone.

The tunnel sloped downward again, the floor growing slicker with algae and grime. Once or twice, Russell's foot slipped; each time, Daniella grabbed him, her fingers digging into his jacket.

"How are you still holding me up?" he asked, half-wondering, half-impressed.

"Adrenaline," she said. "And spite."

"Hot," he muttered.

She elbowed him lightly, trying not to smile while they were literally fleeing sedative gas and a rogue operative.

The sound grew louder.

They rounded a corner—

And the tunnel opened into a massive cylindrical chamber.

Water churned in the center, swirling down like a colossal drain. Rusted catwalks crisscrossed above the whirlpool, leading to maintenance platforms and another tunnel on the far side.

An old stormwater control basin.

"Welcome to the belly of the beast," Rivera mumbled.

Daniella stepped closer to the railing, heart thudding.

"What now?" she asked.

Ashling swept the light along the catwalks.

"There," she said, pointing. "Far side. That tunnel likely

connects to a lower-level service passage. If we can cross—"

A booming echo cracked through the chamber.

A voice followed.

"Going somewhere?"

The sound ricocheted off the curved walls until it felt like it was coming from everywhere.

Ashling stiffened.

Russell's hand found Daniella's again.

Stryker stepped out onto a catwalk above them, gun in hand, raincoat shed, wearing only a dark sweater and black tactical pants.

He looked perfectly at home in the underbelly of the city.

"If you're going to use my escape routes," he said, "at least learn to move faster."

Ashling raised her weapon.

"Don't," he warned. "Ricochets in here are unpredictable. You'll hit one of your own before you hit me."

He started walking along the catwalk, gaze sweeping over them.

"Michael. Still pretending to be the moral one, I see."

Bowman glared. "Still pretending to be human, I see."

Stryker smiled faintly.

His eyes slid to Isla.

"Carrying well?" he asked.

Isla flinched, pressing a hand to her abdomen.

"Stay away from her," Ashling snarled.

"Relax," Stryker said. "The baby is leverage, not a target. I need living proof, not a corpse."

His gaze finally landed on Daniella.

The air around her seemed to thin.

"You," he said quietly. "My favorite complication."

Daniella lifted her chin, heart pounding against her ribs.

"You're afraid of my photographs," she said.

He laughed softly.

"I'm not afraid," he said. "I'm annoyed."

"Because I caught what Mercer didn't want anyone to see," she said. "Because your cleanup wasn't clean."

His smile tightened.

The mask slipped, just slightly.

"Because you don't know how to look away," he said. "That's always the problem with people like you. You think seeing everything makes you powerful. It just makes you useful."

Her skin crawled.

"And what does that make you?" she asked.

His eyes cooled.

"The editor."

Ashling took a step forward. "We're not your story anymore."

"Oh, Ashling," he said. "You always were. A runaway asset. A handler who fell for her cover. A triplet who couldn't keep her family out of her work. You're a disaster of a professional."

His gaze slid to Russell.

"And you," he continued, "were never meant to matter at all. But you do, don't you? To both of them."

Silence slammed through the chamber.

Daniella felt her face flush.

Ashling's fingers tightened on her gun.

Stryker tilted his head.

"Double exposure," he mused. "One man. Two women. One

past. One future. Shame none of it can last. The dam always breaks."

He lifted his gun.

Not at Bowman.

Not at Russell.

Not at Ashling.

At the rusted catwalk supports above the swirling water.

"No!" Ashling shouted.

He fired.

The shot rang like thunder, the sound amplified in the chamber. Metal screamed as one of the suspension joints snapped. The catwalk above them shuddered violently.

"MOVE!" Bowman yelled.

Too late.

The catwalk tore free on one side.

It crashed downward.

Rivera dove away.

Bowman stumbled back.

Isla slammed into the railing.

The impact hit the platform they were standing on like an earthquake. Daniella fell to her knees. Russell lunged toward her—and the floor beneath them buckled.

A section of the platform collapsed.

She grabbed for something, anything. Her fingers found the railing for a split second—

Then air.

Then—

Russell's hand.

He caught her wrist just as the chunk of metal they'd been standing on sheared away and dropped toward the churning water below.

Pain shot through his injured shoulder.

He screamed.

"RUSSELL!" she cried.

He gritted his teeth, holding her weight with everything he had left.

Her body swayed over the whirlpool, mist rising up to bite at her face, water roaring like a hungry throat beneath her.

"Don't... let... go," she gasped.

He laughed weakly. "Not planning on it."

Above, Ashling dropped to her stomach and reached over the crumbling edge, grabbing Russell's other arm just as his grip started to slip.

"I've got you!" she shouted.

"You always do," he grunted.

Daniella dangled between them and the furious water below.

Three people.

One chain.

Stryker watched from the intact catwalk, unreadable.

He could have aimed at any of them.

He didn't.

He holstered his gun instead.

"You're entertaining," he said. "I'll give you that."

"Help us, you bastard!" Rivera yelled.

"Not my job," he replied.

He started walking toward the far tunnel calmly.

Ashling snarled. "Coward!"

He paused.

"Not coward," he said. "Architect."

He looked down at Daniella.

"You're not ready to drown yet," he said quietly. "Not until I see which version of the story you choose to tell."

Then he was gone.

It took everything Russell had left—and everything Ashling had buried in her training—to haul Daniella up inch by inch until she could hook her elbow over the edge.

Rivera and Bowman grabbed her shoulders, helping pull her fully onto the fractured platform.

She collapsed onto the cold metal, chest heaving, fingers shaking uncontrollably.

Russell rolled onto his back, face ashen, eyes squeezed shut against the pain. His bandage was soaked through again.

Ashling knelt, hands hovering over him.

"Idiot," she whispered. "You're a complete idiot."

He cracked one eye open. "You're welcome."

Daniella crawled to his other side, pressing her hands over the worst of the bleeding.

He flinched, then relaxed a fraction under her touch.

"I had you," he murmured.

"You almost didn't," she whispered, voice breaking. "You almost—"

His hand found her cheek weakly.

"But I didn't," he said. "I'm not letting go. Not of you."

Her breath caught.

Ashling's gaze locked on their joined hands, something breaking in her expression.

For a second, Daniella thought she might actually walk away.

Instead, Ashling sat back on her heels and looked straight at Daniella.

"I need you to hear this," she said quietly.

Daniella met her eyes.

"I didn't stumble into your life," Ashling said. "I chose you."

The words hit hard.

"What?" Daniella whispered.

Ashling exhaled.

"Months ago, before you ever met Russell, before that first rooftop shoot, I saw your work," she said. "I was tracking civilian photographers who spent time around federal sites. Most of them got too close and backed off. You didn't. You kept shooting."

Daniella's heart pounded.

"You were looking at me."

"I was looking for someone like you," Ashling said. "Someone who couldn't look away. Someone who didn't know how to stop seeing. Someone whose instincts would get them in trouble... but might save others."

A faint, bitter smile tugged at her mouth.

"In other words, someone like me before they turned me into a weapon."

Daniella's throat burned.

"So you put me with Russell," she said. "Knowing this might happen."

Ashling shook her head.

"I gave the Agency your portfolio," she said. "Told them you'd fit the aesthetic for a tourism campaign. Told them you were clean. Told them you were just good with light."

Her gaze flicked to Russell.

"I didn't know he'd fall for you," she said. "And I didn't know you'd fall back."

Russell blinked between them, dazed. "You... what?"

Ashling swallowed.

"I thought if I attached you to something innocent—a travel campaign, a harmless assignment—it would protect you," she said. "They'd leave you alone. You'd get your art, your cityscapes, your cafes. You'd never see what we really do with places like Rio Dam."

She looked away.

"But you saw anyway. Because you're you. And because I was arrogant enough to think I could control the exposure."

Daniella's eyes stung.

Double exposure.

Ashling's plan.

The Agency's use of her.

Russell's heart.

Her own.

All layered.

All bleeding through.

"Are you sorry?" Daniella whispered.

Ashling's answer was immediate.

"Yes," she said. "For dragging you into a war. For underestimating Stryker. For thinking I could keep you at the edges and you'd never get burned."

She paused.

"But I'm not sorry you met him," she added quietly. "You pulled him back from the edge in ways I never could. He loved me once. He loves you now. That doesn't erase what we had. It just... changes the frame."

Russell swallowed hard.

"Do I get a vote in this?" he rasped.

Ashling's lips twitched. "No. You're shot. Sit down."

He laughed weakly. "Bossy."

Daniella looked between them—the woman who'd chosen her, and the man who kept choosing her even when he shouldn't.

Everything hurt.

Everything mattered.

And for the first time, she realized:

She wasn't just reacting anymore.

She was in the shot.

Not behind the camera.

In front of the world.

A subject and a witness.

"I'm not running," she said softly.

Everyone looked at her.

She lifted her chin.

"I'm tired of being edited," she continued. "By Stryker. By Mercer. Even by whatever plan you thought you had for me, Ashling. If my photos are going to expose them, then I decide how. I decide when. I decide what story we tell."

Rivera smiled slowly. "Now you sound like someone I can put on record."

Bowman nodded once. "Mercer won't see it coming."

Isla wiped her eyes. "My baby won't grow up thinking his father was a traitor."

Ashling held Daniella's gaze.

"Then we finish this," she said.

Together.

Above them, water churned on.

Somewhere in the maze of tunnels, Stryker adjusted his plan, already rewriting the next scene.

But for the first time—

He wasn't the only one composing the story.

CHAPTER 23 – TIES THAT BIND

The stormwater chamber was still groaning from the impact of the fallen catwalk. Metal creaked above them, echoing like the growl of some mechanical beast. Mist curled from the churning water, rising in ghostly tendrils that clung to Daniella's skin as she knelt beside Russell.

He was fading.

Daniella pressed her hand over the soaked bandage on his shoulder. "Stay with me," she whispered.

"I'm trying," Russell murmured, managing a weak, crooked smile. "But you look blurry."

"That's because you're concussed," Isla said gently from the other side. "And because you're stubborn and bleeding."

"I am very stubborn," he said proudly.

Daniella choked out a shaky laugh. "God, you're ridiculous."

Ashling stood near the edge of the broken platform, flashlight sweeping across the catwalk above. Calculating. Assessing. Planning.

Rivera checked her watch. "We need to move before Stryker circles back through one of the upper tunnels."

"Or before Mercer's sweep teams drop into the grid," Bowman added. "He won't let Stryker handle this alone."

Daniella looked up sharply. "Sweep teams?"

Bowman nodded grimly. "Full tactical extraction squads. If Mercer thinks Stryker might fail, he'll send in scorched-earth."

Ashling's jaw hardened. "They won't take Isla alive. Or the baby."

Isla wrapped her arms around herself, shivering. "He knows I'm proof."

"Exactly," Ashling said. "Which means you're valuable until you're not."

Daniella's jaw clenched. "We are not letting them get to her."

Ashling turned. "We? As in, you're making the plans now?"

Daniella inhaled, steadying herself.

"Yes," she said quietly. "I am."

Rivera raised a brow. "Well, damn. She's growing teeth."

Bowman crossed his arms. "Then what do you suggest?"

Daniella stood.

She didn't feel brave.

She felt sick.

Cold.

Terrified.

But fear wasn't a reason to stay quiet anymore.

She pointed toward the far tunnel — the one Stryker disappeared into, the one Ashling previously marked as suspicious.

"That tunnel," she said. "He walked through it without a weapon drawn. He didn't check corners. He didn't scan the room. He wasn't nervous."

Ashling frowned. "Which means?"

"It's not trapped," Daniella said. "Or dangerous. It's controlled."

Bowman nodded slowly. "She's right. Stryker only relaxes when he knows the layout better than anyone else."

Rivera leaned forward. "So you want to follow him?"

Daniella swallowed.

"Yes."

"No."

"You're insane."

"Absolutely not."

The objections came in a chorus from the others.

Daniella held up a hand. "Wait. I'm not saying we chase him. I'm saying that the tunnel connects to something he doesn't want us to find. Something important enough for him to guard but not destroy."

Ashling's expression shifted.

You're not wrong, her eyes seemed to say.

Bowman exhaled through his nose. "If Stryker's using this section as a corridor, odds are it leads to—"

"A maintenance hub," Ashling said.

"Or a comms relay," Rivera added.

"Or," Isla whispered, "a place where he keeps... things."

Everyone froze.

Daniella turned.

"Isla... what do you mean?"

Isla's hands shook. "Hale told me things before he died. Things I didn't understand then. He said Stryker didn't just kill for assignments. He kept evidence. Tokens. Leverage. Proof."

Bowman's shoulders stiffened. "A black archive."

"A private one," Ashling murmured. "Off-books."

Rivera cursed under her breath. "That means files, recordings, footage... maybe every operation he's covered up in a decade."

Daniella's pulse thundered.

"Evidence," she whispered.

The others froze.

Bowman stared at her. "Your photo is one piece. If Stryker has more—actual proof—then Mercer's entire operation collapses."

Ashling nodded slowly. "If we get into Stryker's archive, we could find—"

"The original files," Rivera said.

"Names," Bowman added.

"Locations," Isla whispered.

"Everything," Daniella breathed.

Russell, still half-conscious on the floor, grinned weakly. "Look at you. Acting like a spy."

She kneeled next to him again, brushing a strand of hair off his forehead with trembling fingers.

"I'm acting like myself," she said. "Just with higher stakes."

His smile softened. "Sexy."

"Not helping, Russ."

"Wasn't trying to."

Ashling stepped forward, voice firm:

"If we go after Stryker's archive, we do it smart. Quiet. Fast. The moment he realizes we're anywhere near his files, he'll trigger a purge."

"Meaning?" Rivera asked.

Ashling deadpanned. "He lights the whole place on fire."

Rivera sighed. "Of course he does."

Bowman gestured sharply. "We don't have time to argue. Either we go deeper into the tunnels, or we wait for the sweep teams to pin us in here."

Ashling pointed her flashlight toward the dark mouth of the far tunnel.

"Decision time," she said. "Move now, or die here."

Daniella looked at Isla.

Isla's eyes were wide but steady.

She reached out, gripping Daniella's hand.

"Please," she whispered. "I need... I need to know Hale didn't die a villain. I need his truth. For me. For the baby."

Daniella squeezed her fingers.

"We'll get it," she said. "I promise."

Ashling studied Daniella's face.

For the first time, the admiration wasn't hidden.

"You're braver than you think," Ashling murmured.

Daniella exhaled shakily. "No. I'm just done running."

Bowman stepped beside Ashling. "Lead us."

Ashling nodded.

"Everyone, stay close," she ordered. "Stay quiet. And stay ready."

Russell pushed himself upright. Daniella moved to support him, but he caught her hand before she could.

"I can walk," he said.

"You're hurt."

He gave her a gentle smile. "I walk better when you're beside me."

Her chest tightened.

Ashling's jaw twitched.

Rivera rolled her eyes. "Can you two save the romance for when we're not being hunted by a sociopath?"

Russell smirked. "No promises."

They stepped into the far tunnel.

And for the first time since Rio Dam—

the air felt different.

Colder.

Older.

More intentional.

This wasn't forgotten infrastructure.

This was something built with purpose.

Shadowy alcoves.

Pipes running like veins.

Metal doors sealed shut behind rusted panels.

"This was never on the city plans," Ashling whispered. "Someone hid this."

"Mercer," Bowman said. "Or whoever built RIO before him."

Rivera touched the wall. "Concrete is newer here. Post-2005. Someone reinforced this place."

They followed the slope downward, Daniella and Russell in the middle, Isla leaning on Rivera, and Bowman covering the rear.

Halfway down the tunnel, Daniella felt it—

A faint vibration beneath her feet.

She paused.

"What is it?" Russell murmured.

She lowered her body, pressing her fingertips to the concrete.

A hum traveled up her arm.

Like electricity.

Like machinery.

"A generator," she whispered.

Ashling crouched beside her. "You sure?"

Daniella nodded. "My dad used to bring home broken electronics and have me help fix them. I know the feel of a running circuit."

Ashling stared at her for three long seconds.

Then—

A slow, stunned smile.

"What?" Daniella whispered.

"I spent years training operatives to read environments," Ashling said softly. "And somehow you naturally do half of it without knowing you're doing it."

Daniella's cheeks warmed.

Rivera stepped closer.

"Alright, prodigy. You tell us—where's it coming from?"

Daniella closed her eyes, feeling the vibration shift through the floor.

She turned her palm slightly.

"Left," she said. "Below us."

Bowman exhaled. "Maintenance bay."

Ashling nodded. "Stryker's archive would need power."

Daniella pushed to her feet. "Then that's where we go."

They followed the vibration through a tight corridor that bent sharply to the left. Then the right. The hum grew stronger. Louder. More insistent.

Finally—

They reached a steel door marked with peeling black paint.

No label.

No lock panel.

Just a seam in the metal.

Ashling pressed her ear to it.

Nothing.

She nodded at Bowman.

He raised his gun.

She counted silently—

3... 2... 1—

Bowman kicked the door with everything he had left.

It buckled inward, metal screaming.

And the moment it gave way—

Every breath froze.

The room beyond was lined with metal cabinets, servers stacked in rows like tombstones, hard drives blinking in the dim light, old monitors cycling through surveillance feeds—

Footage of tunnels.

Of alleys.

Of rooms.

Of Daniella's studio.

Of the Rio Dam.

Of Ashling.

Of Bowman.

Of…

Daniella.

Her breath shattered.

This was it.

Stryker's archive.

A library of sins.

Ashling stepped inside slowly, flashlight drifting over the rows.

"This is years," she whispered. "Years of operations. Years of blackmail. Years of leverage."

Bowman's face hardened. "We can bring Mercer down with this."

Rivera nodded. "And get the truth about Hale."

Isla clutched Daniella's arm. "Go. Find something about him. Please."

Daniella moved down the nearest row, heart pounding. Old Manila folders. USB sticks. Labeled tapes. Unlabeled drives. Everything organized with clinical precision.

She stopped at the sight of a metal case labeled:

H–117 / Asset Termination / RIO

Her throat tightened.

"Hale," she whispered.

Russell reached for her hand, steadying her.

Ashling approached another cabinet, pausing at a separate box:

M-001 / Director Review / RIO

Her eyebrows shot up.

"Mercer," she breathed.

Bowman's voice came from across the room.

"Grab what you can. We leave in five."

Daniella turned back to the Hale case, hands trembling.

She unlatched the lid.

Inside were documents.

Photos.

A USB drive.

And—

Her breath caught.

A sealed envelope.

Marked in Hale's handwriting.

For Isla.

"Isla," Daniella whispered. "Come here."

Isla rushed over, eyes wide with a kind of grief Daniella had never seen before.

Daniella placed the envelope in her hands gently.

Isla broke.

She sobbed, sinking to her knees, holding the letter to her chest like it was Hale himself.

Ashling knelt beside her, wrapping an arm around her sister.

Rivera blinked quickly, looking away, clearing her throat.

Bowman pretended not to notice.

Russell squeezed Daniella's hand.

"You did that," he whispered. "You got her that."

Daniella swallowed, tears burning her eyes. "It's not enough."

"It's the beginning," he murmured.

Suddenly—

The overhead lights flickered.

Everyone froze.

Bowman cursed.

"Stryker triggered the purge," Ashling barked.

Rivera sprinted to one of the servers. "Files are being deleted—systemically."

Bowman grabbed drives. "Take everything physical!"

Ashling yanked open drawers. "Copy nothing—grab originals!"

Daniella shoved folders into her bag with shaking hands.

Russell leaned heavily against a cabinet, face pale.

Ashling looked over at him. "He's crashing. Daniella—"

"I know," she said. "Hold on, Russ. Please."

He nodded weakly.

Rivera pulled the last drive free. "That's it! Move!"

Ashling grabbed Isla. "Stay with me—don't look back."

Bowman waved them forward.

Daniella looked back just once.

Rows of files—

Years of secrets—

Everything—

Beginning to burn from within as the purge sequence activated, sparks popped across the racks.

Stryker's legacy erasing itself.

As if it had never existed.

She turned and ran.

The corridor shook.

Heat bloomed.

Sparks flew.

Bowman yelled, "MOVE!"

They sprinted toward the tunnel mouth, the roar of collapsing metal chasing them.

Daniella grabbed Russell's arm—

He stumbled—

She caught him—

Ashling pulled them both forward—

Isla ran beside them, clutching Hale's letter—

Rivera sprinted ahead—

Bowman shielded the rear—

They burst out into the main tunnel as fire exploded from the chamber behind them.

Daniella hit the ground hard, Russell collapsing beside her.

Ashling slammed the door shut.

Bowman threw his weight against it.

The blast rattled the corridor.

Then—

Silence.

Real silence.

Breathing.

Crying.

Coughing.

Alive.

Russell rolled onto his back, breathing hard. "I hate tunnels."

Daniella let out a shaky laugh.

Then leaned over him—

Pressed her forehead to his—

"We're okay," she whispered. "We're okay."

He lifted a trembling hand.

Touched her cheek.

"You are," he murmured. "You're more than okay."

Her heart cracked open.

Behind them, Isla clutched her envelope like a lifeline.

Ashling watched Daniella and Russell, jealousy flickering—

then fading.

Replaced by something accepting.

Painful, but real.

Bowman stood, bruised and bleeding, but resolute.

Rivera tucked the stolen drive into her jacket. "This? This brings them down."

Daniella sat back, breath shaking, adrenaline fading.

"What now?" she asked.

Rivera smiled grimly.

"Now, sweetheart?"

She tapped the metal case holding Mercer's files.

Now we expose the whole damn truth."

Rivera smiled grimly.

"Now," she said, "we tell your story before Mercer writes the ending."

CHAPTER 24 – BOWMAN'S DISCOVERY

They didn't stop moving until they reached the surface.

Two blocks from Rivera's hideout, through a rusted iron grate hidden beneath a pile of trash bags, the group hauled itself into a narrow basement corridor of an abandoned textile warehouse. Dust motes danced in the sliver of morning light slicing through a broken window.

Bowman sealed the grate behind them with a length of pipe.

Rivera locked the storage door from the inside.

Ashling checked her weapon, her breathing sharp and controlled.

Daniella leaned Russell against the wall. He slid down to sit, grimacing as the pain flared in his shoulder.

Isla took a shaky breath and finally unfolded the envelope Hale had left for her.

Bowman set his bag on an old wooden table in the center of the room.

And he opened the case.

THE FILES

Mercer's files weren't electronic.

Not all of them.

Some were typed on yellowing paper.

Some were old photographs.

Others were handwritten memos with coffee stains and the edges worn soft.

A history built on paper cuts and buried truths.

Bowman pulled out a folder marked:

RIO – GENESIS

Classified — Eyes Only

Daniella watched his eyes as he unfolded the first sheet.

His expression changed.

Something inside him broke — or hardened.

Rivera stepped beside him. "What is it?"

Bowman exhaled. "It started earlier than we thought."

Ashling moved closer. "How early?"

Bowman held up the memo.

Ashling sucked in a breath. Isla covered her mouth. Daniella felt her stomach twist.

June 2001

Subject: RIO Protocol — Foundational Initiative

Director: J. Mercer

Purpose: Civilian Integration and Behavioral Capture through Indirect Surveillance.

Phase One Objective: Identify civilians capable of involuntary intelligence extraction.

Rivera frowned. "What the hell does that mean?"

Bowman's voice dropped.

Quiet.

Sickened.

Knowing.

"Mercer wasn't building a strike unit," he said. "He was building an observer net. Civilians with exceptional perceptual instincts. Photographers. Artists. Journalists. People who see things others don't."

Daniella's pulse spiked.

Ashling whispered it before Daniella could.

"People like her."

Bowman nodded.

"People exactly like Daniella."

Daniella stepped back a half-step, chest tightening. "What are you talking about?"

Bowman slid another page toward her.

Target Identification Sub-Program — Civilian Watchers

Criteria:

– High visual acuity

– Pattern recognition instinct

– Habitual documentation

– Involuntary proximity to federal operations

– Psychological profiles indicating persistence, curiosity, and obsession with detail

Daniella stared at the words hard enough that they blurred.

Ashling shut her eyes. "He wasn't looking for spies. He was looking for eyes."

Bowman turned the page.

A list.

Names.

Dozens of them.

At the bottom of the second column:

Russo, Daniella — Priority Candidate

Daniella's knees nearly gave out.

Russell caught her with his good hand. "Hey. Hey—look at me."

Her breath shook. "They... they were watching me?"

"For years," Rivera said quietly. "Before you even knew Russell. Before you met Ashling."

Daniella swallowed hard. "Why?"

Bowman lifted another document.

This one was a psychological profile.

Her psychological profile.

The heading read:

Case Study — Civilian Watcher Candidate (DR-07)

Subject: Russo, Daniella

Notes:

– Strong observational instincts

– Demonstrates unconscious pattern analysis

– Captures unintended intelligence in photographic work

– Zero awareness of involvement

– Recommended for integration through benign cover assignments

Ashling's voice dropped to a whisper.

"That's why the travel campaign was approved. That's why they placed it in front of Russell. That's why they greenlit the entire project."

Daniella stared at them.

"What do you mean, placed it in front of Russell?" she asked quietly.

Ashling met her eyes — guilt visible, raw, painful.

"It wasn't a coincidence," she said. "The Agency received a request for a local photographer. I gave them your portfolio."

Daniella went cold.

"You... you put me in this?"

Ashling's eyes glistened. "I thought it would protect you. I thought if they had a role for you—something small and innocent—you'd stay off their radar. Away from RIO."

Daniella shook her head. "Ashling... I trusted you."

"I know," Ashling whispered. "I know."

Russell's hand tightened around Daniella's.

But Daniella gently pulled her hand back.

Not away from Russell.

Away from the truth, crushing the air from her lungs.

She turned to Bowman. "Keep going."

Bowman hesitated. "Daniella—"

"KEEP GOING."

He unfolded another sheet.

This one was dated two days before Hale died.

Directive: Field Termination — H. Hale

Reason: Compromised assets, risk of exposing RIO civilian integration strategy

Agent Assigned: C. Stryker

Operative Present: J. Mercer

Secondary Objective:

Recover evidence from Artist Russo if captured.

If not, neutralize and acquire film.

Daniella's breath left her body in a single violent exhale.

"They were going to kill me," she whispered.

Bowman nodded. "Yes."

Ashling slammed her fist onto the table so hard the entire case rattled. "You were NEVER supposed to see this. I thought—God, Daniella, I thought I had kept you out of this."

Daniella stared at the page again.

Her name.

In Mercer's handwriting.

As part of a termination directive.

Russell pulled himself upright, leaning heavily on the table.

"Mercer wanted her silenced so the photo wouldn't come out," he growled. "Hale knew something. He tried to pass it to Isla. Stryker stopped him. Daniella caught him in the frame."

Rivera nodded slowly, eyes sharpening. "She saw what she wasn't supposed to. And she saw who she wasn't supposed to."

Bowman slid the biggest file in the box toward them.

Its label:

MERCER — BLACK OPERATIONS — CONFIDENTIAL

Ashling opened it.

Inside were dozens of photographs.

Most of them surveillance.

Some dated back years.

Some were stamped with Hale's initials.

Some with Stryker's.

But one—

One made every head in the room snap forward.

A photo from years ago.

Director Mercer standing beside a young woman.

A woman with a damaged file number.

A woman missing from any Agency roster.

Ashling froze.

Rivera whispered, "Oh God…"

Isla gasped, hand flying to her mouth.

Russell inhaled sharply.

Daniella whispered, "Who is she?"

Bowman answered in a low, horrified voice:

"Ashling. That's your sister."

Ashling's entire body went rigid.

"No," she whispered. "My sister died in a fire. Years ago. I identified her. I—"

Bowman shook his head.

"No. You identified a burned corpse with a partial DNA match. Mercer falsified the rest."

Ashling stared at the photo, trembling.

Her lost triplet.

Alive.

Standing beside Mercer.

"She was never dead," Bowman said. "She was recruited."

"Ashling…" Isla whispered, tears spilling over. "He took her."

Ashling staggered back, pain crumpling her face.

Daniella stepped toward her.

But Ashling lifted a hand, shaking her head.

"No," she whispered. "No. I can't—"

Bowman pulled out another sheet from the bottom of the file.

A recent report.

Dated last week.

Target: A. Moore

Status: Recovered

Under Directive: Field Reassignment

Location: RIO Facility — Sector 4

Ashling's knees nearly buckled.

Daniella grabbed her before she fell.

Rivera looked between them. "If Sector 4 holds your sister... then that's where Mercer is keeping everything."

Bowman nodded grimly. "Sector 4 is less than an hour outside the city. A black site. No outside access."

Ashling whispered, "I thought she was dead. I thought she was—"

Daniella held her tighter. "Ashling... we'll find her."

Ashling's voice cracked. "You can't promise that."

Daniella met her eyes.

"Yes," she whispered. "I can."

Russell leaned forward, voice tight and cold. "Then we hit Sector 4. We take Mercer down. We get Ashling's sister. We clear Isla. We stop Stryker. And we give Daniella back her life."

Bowman nodded.

Rivera smirked. "Now this is a story."

Daniella inhaled slowly.

For the first time—

She wasn't the hunted.

She was the one with the truth.

And she knew exactly where she needed to take it.

She stepped to the table, looked at the files, then at the people around her.

Fear still clung to her ribs.

But beneath it—

Something harder.

Hotter.

Sharpening.

Resolve.

"We go after Mercer," she said. "Tonight."

The room went still.

Ashling wiped her eyes. "You're sure?"

Daniella nodded. "Because I'm done being their pawn."

Bowman's mouth twitched. "Then let's move."

Isla stood beside them, still clutching Hale's letter. "We do it for him."

"For your baby," Daniella said.

Isla nodded.

Rivera crossed her arms. "For the story that takes them down."

Ashling's eyes darkened with newfound fire. "For my sister."

Russell met Daniella's gaze, gripping her hand.

"And for us," he whispered.

Daniella swallowed the emotion rising in her throat.

"Yes," she whispered. "For us."

Bowman grabbed the box.

"Sector 4," he said. "Time to burn RIO to the ground."

CHAPTER 25 – THE BETRAYAL

Sector 4 wasn't on any map.

Not the official ones, not the city's digital records, not even the classified lists Rivera had spent years hacking through. It was buried so deeply inside the government's black-budget labyrinth that even Bowman only knew rumors:

No windows. No public records. No jurisdiction besides RIO itself.

The kind of place you get erased into.

The kind of place Mercer could hide anything—or anyone.

Russell leaned against Daniella as the team moved through the abandoned warehouse district at the edge of the city. His injured shoulder throbbed, his steps uneven, but he refused help beyond the pressure of Daniella's hand around his waist.

"You should rest," she whispered.

He breathed a laugh that broke into a wince. "I rest when this is over. Or when you stop looking at me like I might die."

"Russell—"

He pressed his forehead to hers. "I'm here. I'm not going anywhere."

Ashling cleared her throat sharply. "Move. Both of you.

Preferably with less... whatever that is."

Daniella stepped back, embarrassed.

Ashling didn't look at her.

Didn't look at Russell either.

Her jaw was locked, her movements sharp enough to cut.

Bowman scanned the perimeter with binoculars. "Sector 4 sits under the old Cold Valley Logistics compound. Five stories aboveground, fifteen below. Most of it automated. Very little foot staff."

Rivera cracked her knuckles. "Electric grid?"

"Redundant. Triple-backed."

Daniella frowned. "Meaning?"

"Meaning," Rivera said, "they built this place assuming the government might someday try to shut it down."

Ashling paced, eyes narrowing. "We can't brute-force our way in. We'll need the central access codes."

"And you know where they are," Bowman said.

Ashling stopped pacing.

Her breath hitched.

"The Director's office," she whispered.

Daniella stepped closer. "Mercer keeps the access inside his private wing?"

Ashling nodded. "Only three people have access to those codes. Mercer, Stryker, and..."

Her voice trailed off.

Something flickered behind her eyes.

Bowman stiffened. "Ashling?"

She swallowed.

"There's one more."

Her voice cracked.

"My sister."

Silence smothered the group.

Russell ran a hand through his hair. "So she was high-ranking enough to—"

"No," Ashling snapped. "No, she was used enough. Groomed enough. Controlled enough."

Isla stepped forward, clutching Hale's letter, her eyes wide with something between fear and heartbreak.

"Ashling... we're going to get her back."

Ashling turned away.

Daniella walked to her, gently touching her arm.

"We're doing this for her," Daniella whispered. "Not just for the files. Not just for Hale. For your family."

Ashling's jaw trembled.

She nodded once.

Hard.

"Then let's move."

THE MAP THEY WEREN'T SUPPOSED TO HAVE

Rivera unfolded the crude map she'd sketched from memory—underground tunnels, security choke points, chemical vents, substations.

Every path a risk.

Every shortcut a trap.

"We hit from the east," Rivera said. "Fewer cameras."

"That still gets us inside the perimeter," Bowman said. "But after that... we improvise."

"Improvising is how people die," Ashling said coldly.

Bowman met her eyes. "It's also how people get out."

Isla tucked Hale's letter into her jacket and stepped forward, surprising everyone when she spoke:

"Stop fighting."

All heads turned.

Isla's hands trembled, but her voice didn't.

"Hale died because people who were supposed to work together got too caught in their own missions," she said. "We're not making that mistake."

Rivera blinked. "Kid's got fire."

"She always did," Ashling whispered.

Russell reached for Daniella's hand.

She took it.

And for one moment—

The team felt united.

Hopeful.

Determined.

Then—

Behind them—

A soft click.

Not loud.

But unmistakable.

A gun being cocked.

They spun.

Bowman's pistol was raised.

But not at a target.

At them.

Daniella's breath froze.

Ashling's eyes widened.

Russell stepped in front of Daniella.

Bowman didn't lower the gun.

His voice was hollow.

"Put your hands where I can see them."

"Mike," Rivera snapped. "What the hell—"

He didn't blink.

"Do it," Bowman said. "Now."

Ashling's eyes went flat and deadly as she slowly raised her hands.

"You've got three seconds to explain this before I decide you've lost your mind," she hissed.

Bowman swallowed.

Pain flashed across his face.

"It's me," he whispered. "I'm the one who led him here."

The world tilted.

Daniella felt her stomach drop.

"Mike…" Ashling breathed.

Russell clenched his fists. "You're working with Stryker?"

Bowman's voice cracked.

"No. Not him. Mercer."

Silence detonated like a bomb.

Daniella's pulse hammered. "You… you betrayed us?"

Bowman's eyes filled with regret.

"You don't understand," he said, shaking. "He has my son."

Ashling stared. "You don't have a son."

Bowman's voice broke.

"I didn't know I had a son. Not until Mercer showed me proof two months ago. The mother was a CI on a trafficking case fifteen years ago. I never—"

His voice faltered.

"He sent me a picture. A boy. Looks just like me. Mercer said if

I ever turned on RIO, if I ever went too deep—he'd vanish. No trace."

Daniella felt her throat tighten.

"Mike..." she whispered.

He lifted the gun again, steady hands despite the tremor in his voice.

"I didn't want this. But Mercer knew this operation was collapsing. He ordered a fallback. Told me to drive you into Sector 4. Contain you until Stryker arrives."

Ashling snarled. "And then what? Kill us?"

Bowman flinched. "Not you. Not Isla. Or Rivera. But... Daniella..."

Daniella's breath stopped.

Russell stepped closer, shielding her.

Bowman's eyes filled with tears.

"He said the girl dies tonight."

Ashling lunged—but froze when Bowman's gun snapped toward her.

"Don't," Bowman whispered. "I can't... I can't let him hurt my son."

Daniella stepped forward slowly.

Everyone shouted—

"Daniella!"

"No—stay back!"

"He'll shoot—"

She ignored them.

She walked until the barrel was inches from her heart.

Bowman shook violently.

"Don't do this," he whispered.

"You're not going to shoot me," she said softly.

"You don't know that."

"I do."

She stepped closer.

Bowman sobbed.

"I can't lose him."

"You won't," she whispered. "We're going to get him back. You are not alone. Mercer is lying. He's using you the same way he used Ashling's sister. The same way he used Hale. The same way he tried to use me."

His hand wavered.

Daniella lifted her hand—

And wrapped her fingers around the barrel.

Bowman squeezed his eyes shut.

"I'm so sorry," he choked.

Ashling moved.

Fast.

Silent.

Precise.

Her hand snapped forward.

A nerve strike to Bowman's wrist.

The gun clattered to the concrete.

Bowman collapsed to his knees, sobbing into his hands.

Ashling shoved the gun away with her foot and grabbed his collar.

"You stupid, desperate, loyal idiot," she whispered harshly. "You should have told us."

Russell's breath came unevenly. "Mike... Mike, look at me."

Bowman didn't.

Russell crouched in front of him, ignoring the pain in his

shoulder.

"You're not our enemy."

Bowman looked up, face wet with tears.

"You'll never trust me again."

"Don't give me orders," Russell said fiercely. "You've kept us alive for days. That counts."

Rivera crossed her arms. "He betrayed us because Mercer threatened a child. Every parent on earth understands that."

Isla knelt beside him gently. "We'll rescue him, too."

Bowman stared at her, broken. "You don't even know him."

"You don't have to know someone to save them," she whispered.

Ashling exhaled shakily and released his jacket.

"Next time," she said, "you tell me. Before you point a gun at the woman I dragged into this godforsaken mess."

Daniella stepped forward.

Bowman looked up at her, expectation of hatred in his eyes.

She didn't hate him.

She knelt—slowly—and placed her hand against his cheek.

"We'll go get your son," she whispered. "Together."

Bowman broke.

He dropped his head against her shoulder, hands shaking, breath coming in ragged gasps.

Russell looked at Daniella like she'd just done something impossible.

Ashling's jaw flexed in a way that was neither jealousy nor anger—

But respect.

Rivera wiped her eyes. "Well. Now that the emotional bomb has exploded… can we get back to taking down RIO?"

Bowman wiped his face.

Stood.

And nodded sharply.

"I'm with you," he said.

Daniella looked toward the looming direction of the hidden facility—Sector 4.

"Then let's finish this."

She lifted Mercer's file.

Lifted Hale's case.

Lifted her camera bag.

Lifted her resolve.

"And let's save everyone he stole."

CHAPTER 26 – UNDER FIRE

Sector 4 rose out of the earth like a concrete scar—cold, massive, windowless, and humming with hidden life beneath the surface. You couldn't stumble onto this place. You had to know exactly where it was buried.

Now they did.

Rivera crouched beside a broken retaining wall, peering through binoculars.

"Three ground patrols. Automatics. Their sweeps are tight, but they're not expecting anyone on foot."

Bowman scanned the perimeter with the focused calm of a man who'd spent half his life walking into gunfire. "They think the tunnels are still purging. Stryker probably told Mercer the job's done."

Ashling checked her weapon. "Meaning we're ghosts until we break something."

Russell leaned heavily against a tree, pain dancing under his skin like fire. He tried to hide it, but Daniella saw everything.

She stepped closer, lowering her voice. "Talk to me."

"I'm fine," Russell said—lying, badly.

"Your shoulder's bleeding again."

"I've had worse."

"Russell—"

He reached for her hand. His fingers were cold.

"Told you. I walk better when you're next to me."

Her heart twisted.

But Ashling's voice snapped the moment.

"Putting the romance on hold," she said. "We're going in."

Bowman pointed to a narrow concrete drainage channel near the base of the facility. "Rivera, that grate still leads into sub-level vent corridors?"

"Yep. Maintenance tunnels. Mostly forgotten. I've crawled through tighter spaces, avoiding ex-boyfriends."

Isla blinked. "That... is oddly specific."

"Not the time," Ashling said.

Daniella swallowed and looked at the massive structure ahead.

Sector 4.

Where Ashling's sister was being held.

Where Mercer kept his deepest secrets.

Where RIO began—and where it needed to end.

Russell touched her shoulder. "Stay near me."

She nodded.

Ashling gestured sharply. "Teams of two. Move fast. No improvising. No heroics."

Rivera smirked. "So... heroics?"

Ashling glared.

"For once—no."

Bowman took point.

Ashling and Isla followed.

Rivera dropped down the slope next.

And Daniella and Russell brought up the rear, staying close as they moved along the tree line.

But before they reached the grate—

Russell faltered.

His step buckled.

His breath hitched sharply.

His knees almost gave out.

Daniella grabbed him, panic slicing through her.

"Russ—Russ! Hey—don't do this. Look at me."

He tried to straighten.

Failed.

"It's... the blood loss," he said. "I just need a second—"

Ashling turned.

And froze.

Not at Russell.

But at the tree line behind them.

Her voice dropped lower than Daniella had ever heard.

"Move."

Bowman raised his gun. "Ashling—"

"MOVE!"

But it was already too late.

A soft phffft cut the air.

A tranquilizer dart slammed into the tree trunk inches from Daniella's head.

Bowman yelled, "CONTACT!"

Before they could react—

Enforcers flooded out of the trees.

Black tactical suits.

Night-vision visors.

Suppressors glowing faint green.

Mercer's sweep team.

They'd been waiting.

Watching.

Hunting.

Russell shoved Daniella behind him just as automatic fire erupted.

Ashling fired first.

Bowman second.

Rivera dove behind a boulder, returning fire.

Daniella hit the dirt, adrenaline flooding her veins.

Russell dragged her toward the grate, his blood leaving a crimson smear across the gravel.

"Go!" he shouted. "Get in!"

"No—I'm not leaving you!"

"Daniella—GO!"

Another dart hit the ground inches from her knee.

She felt heat rush through her chest.

Ashling threw her a sidearm. "Use it!"

Daniella caught the gun without thinking—hands steady, instincts automatic.

Russell looked at her as if seeing her for the first time.

Then—

A grenade hit the ground nearby.

A concussive shockwave ripped through the air.

Dust and dirt exploded upward.

Daniella's ears rang violently.

Her vision blurred.

Russell collapsed to one knee, groaning.

Through the haze, Daniella saw Isla screaming.

Rivera firing with deadly precision.

Bowman dragging Isla backward.

Ashling covering them with expert, brutal calm.

Everything was chaos.

And then—

The real nightmare began.

A spotlight snapped on above the facility.

A voice—smooth, amplified, familiar—echoed over hidden speakers.

"Stand down. All of you."

Daniella froze.

Russell looked up, rage twisting his features.

Ashling's eyes went murderous.

Bowman went still.

Rivera whispered, "No... no no no—"

Because the voice—

The voice belonged to Director James Mercer.

And he sounded amused.

"You've fought well," Mercer said. "But this ends now."

Enforcers tightened their formation.

Weapons raised.

Dot sights painting red glows across the ground—and across the team.

Mercer continued:

"Step away from the girl."

Daniella's breath caught.

He didn't say the group.

He didn't say the fugitives.

He said:

"The girl."

Russell growled, "Over my dead body."

Mercer chuckled.

"That, Russell, can be arranged."

Daniella's heart hammered.

"Why me?" she shouted. "Why are you doing this?"

Mercer answered softly, cold as steel:

"Because you saw something you were never meant to see.

Because you were built for RIO even before we found you.

And because you're the only loose end I cannot afford."

Ashling screamed, "MERCER!"

A volley of shots answered.

They hit the dirt again.

Mercer's voice hardened to ice.

"Take the girl alive. Eliminate the rest."

Russell shoved Daniella toward the grate. "Run!"

"Not without you!"

"GO!"

She pulled at him—but his strength faltered again.

A tranquilizer dart hit Russell's thigh.

He gasped, grabbing the tree to stay upright.

"No—Russell!" Daniella cried.

He tried to stand.

Failed.

Eyes heavy.

Hands shaking.

"Dani…" he whispered. "I'm not… leaving you…"

But he was going down.

Right there.

Right before her.

Before she could save him.

Ashling grabbed Daniella's arm. "We have to MOVE!"

Daniella fought her, screaming, "NO! RUSSELL!"

But Bowman and Rivera were pulling Isla into the tunnel.

Gunfire rained around them.

The grate entrance was seconds from being overrun.

Daniella reached for Russell—

He reached back—

Their fingers brushed—

And then—

Stryker stepped into the clearing.

Alive.

Armed.

Smiling.

He grabbed Russell by the collar.

Daniella screamed as Stryker lifted Russell's limp body.

Stryker's voice was a dagger to her heart.

"See you inside, sweetheart."

Then he dragged Russell toward Sector 4.

The tranquilizer hit Daniella's leg a split second later.

Her vision dimmed.

Her body went weak.

Her scream died in her throat.

Ashling caught her before she hit the ground—

"NO—NO—DANI—WAKE UP—I NEED YOU—"

Daniella fought consciousness, clawing at the air.

"R...russ..."

Her world dissolved.

Her last thought was a whisper:

Don't let him take him. Don't let him...

Then darkness swallowed her.

CHAPTER 27 — THE FINAL FILE

Darkness wasn't silent.

It pulsed.

It hummed.

It breathed around her like a living thing.

Daniella floated in it—weightless, numb, her body refusing to obey. She felt herself sink, rise, drift. Heard echoes that didn't belong to her.

"Take the girl alive."

"Russell!—No!"

"Goodnight, sweetheart."

"Dani—wake up—Dani—"

Then—

A sound cut through it.

Beep.

Beep.

Rhythmic. Mechanical.

Her eyes snapped open.

The world sharpened with painful clarity.

Cold steel walls.

Fluorescent lights humming overhead.

A small metal bed beneath her.

A glass wall in front of her—thick enough to survive an explosion.

Daniella swallowed hard.

Sector 4.

She was inside it.

Her arm ached. A tiny puncture wound marked where they injected her. Her clothes were gone, replaced with a gray facility shirt and loose cotton pants.

She forced herself to sit up.

Her head pounded.

Her leg throbbed where the second dart hit.

But none of it mattered.

Because her first thought was—

Where is Russell?

Her heart slammed in her chest as she leaned against the glass, peering out into a brightly lit corridor.

Empty.

Cold.

Silent.

"Russell?" she whispered, her voice shaking. "Russ? RUSSELL!"

No answer.

She pressed her forehead to the glass, tears burning her eyes.

Please... please be alive.

A soft hiss broke the silence.

A door sliding open.

She spun.

Footsteps approached down the hall.

Measured. Calm.

Confident.

A tall man stepped into view, silhouetted by the sterile lights behind him.

Director James Mercer.

Wearing a tailored suit. Not a wrinkle out of place. A man who could watch the world burn and call it policy.

He smiled—soft and polite.

Like she was a guest.

"Miss Russo," he said warmly. "You're finally awake."

Daniella's fingers curled into fists. "Where is he?"

Mercer clasped his hands behind his back, strolling as though they walked in a museum.

"Russell Kane is alive," he said. "For now."

Her chest tightened. "If you hurt him—"

"I haven't," Mercer interrupted. "Stryker simply... sedated him. Rest assured, he's being taken care of."

"Taken care of?" Daniella hissed. "You're torturing him, aren't you? Like you tortured Hale. Like you—"

"Miss Russo," Mercer said with a sigh, "your conclusions are becoming exhausting. I didn't bring you here to upset you. I brought you here because you are the only person who can finish RIO."

Daniella froze.

"What?" she whispered.

Mercer stopped directly in front of the glass wall separating them.

He lifted a tablet and pressed it to the glass.

The device lit up with a familiar image.

Her photograph.

The one she took at the dam—the one Ashling said captured something no one was meant to see.

Mercer zoomed in.

Not on Hale.

Not on Ashling.

Not on the shadows.

But on the frame structure itself. The angle. The composition.

"This image," Mercer said, "is not an accident. It is a blueprint."

Daniella's mouth went dry. "A blueprint for what?"

Mercer looked at her with something like admiration.

"For pattern detection. For algorithmic intelligence mapping. You captured the moment our operation intersected with civilian world space in a way our analysts could never replicate."

Daniella shook her head. "I just took a picture."

"No," Mercer said softly. "You saw. Really saw. You captured multiple layers of intelligence in a single frame without knowing what you were doing."

He tapped the glass.

"This image changes everything."

Daniella stared at him, horror slowly sinking in.

"You built RIO... around me?"

Mercer smiled. "Around people like you, yes. You are the perfect civilian observer. Curious. Persistent. Detached yet emotionally connected in just the right measure."

He leaned closer.

"You are what we've been trying to create for decades."

Daniella stepped back, breath shaking. "I'm a photographer. That's it."

Mercer shook his head. "Oh, my dear girl... you're so much more."

A scream echoed from deeper within the facility.

A woman's scream.

Pained.

Familiar.

Daniella's blood ran cold.

"Ashling," she whispered.

Mercer raised a brow. "Ah. Yes. Your... ally."

Daniella lunged toward the glass, palms slamming against it. "Where is she?!"

Mercer sighed. "I warned her for years. She never listens."

"What did you do to her?!"

"I didn't do anything."

Mercer paused.

A sinister smile curled across his lips.

"She asked to see her sister."

Daniella froze.

Her heart dropped.

"No," she whispered. "No—Mercer, don't—"

"Too late."

He tapped another button on the tablet.

The screen changed.

A live feed appeared.

Ashling stood inside another glass chamber—just like Daniella's.

She was shaking.

Crying.

Her hands pressed to the glass.

Across from her—

In the next chamber—

A woman stood motionless.

Same dark hair.

Same jawline.

Same eyes, except empty.

Ashling's lost triplet.

Alive.

Broken.

Unrecognizing.

"Ashling..." Daniella whispered, tears spilling down her cheeks.

Mercer tilted his head. "Remarkable, isn't it? Trauma does fascinating things to the mind. Unfortunately, she doesn't remember Ashling. She doesn't remember herself. She only remembers RIO."

Ashling pressed her forehead to the glass, sobbing.

"Lina... Lina, it's me. It's Ash... please... look at me..."

Her sister only stared blankly.

Mercer turned back to Daniella.

"This is why we built RIO. To mold minds. To shape behavior. To create perfect assets."

"You're a monster," Daniella whispered.

"Perhaps," Mercer said calmly. "But effective."

Daniella's fists shook with rage.

Mercer didn't blink.

"And now, Miss Russo, you will help me finish what we started. You will unlock the final sequence. You will give RIO its future."

"I will never help you."

Mercer smiled as though she were a child making a predictable mistake.

"You will."

He stepped aside.

Stryker dragged Russell into view.

Bound.

Barely conscious.

Blood dried along his jaw.

Daniella screamed, slamming her fists against the glass.

"RUSSELL!"

His head lifted weakly.

"Dani..." he whispered.

Stryker smirked.

Mercer clasped his hands neatly.

"You will help us, Miss Russo. Or the man you love dies in front of you."

Daniella's breath shattered.

Her world collapsed.

Mercer leaned in close to the glass, eyes bright with victory.

"Now," he whispered. "Shall we begin?"

CHAPTER 28 – THE LAST PHOTOGRAPH

Daniella had never known real fear until now.

Not the creeping kind, not anxiety or dread—

—but the kind that swallowed the world whole.

She stood frozen in her glass cell as Stryker held a limp, bloodied Russell by the collar, forcing him upright for Mercer to admire.

"This is crude, even for you," she spat.

Mercer smiled, unmoved.

"Pain is a universal motivator. Russell is simply... incentive."

"He's dying," she growled.

"Yes," Mercer said, completely unfazed. "Which is why your cooperation is now critical."

Her hands shook with rage.

"Let him go."

"After," Mercer said. "Once you give me what I need."

Stryker shoved Russell to his knees. He caught himself with one hand, groaning.

"Dani..." he murmured. "Don't... don't do anything... for me..."

She pressed her palm against the glass.

"I'm not losing you."

Russell's eyes lifted to hers, blurred but fierce.

"You're stronger than this... stronger than them..."

Mercer rapped lightly on the glass, interrupting.

"Let's begin."

He tapped a code into the panel beside her cell.

The opposite wall slid open with a hydraulic hiss.

Another room was revealed on the other side—white, empty, sterile, except for a single metal table and a camera mounted overhead.

A photo studio.

Daniella was stunned.

Mercer gestured to the table.

On it lay a spread of photographs—her photographs—taken over the last weeks.

"Miss Russo," Mercer said softly, "you have a gift. Not just for composition or timing... but for unconscious intelligence capture."

She glared at him. "Stop calling it that. They're just pictures."

He chuckled, amused.

"Oh, no. Not to us."

He lifted one of her prints and pressed it against the glass.

The picture she took at Rio Dam.

At first glance, nothing special.

She'd thought it was just a beautiful shot.

But Mercer zoomed into the corner.

There—between the shadows—was something she'd never noticed.

A reflection.

A metallic grid.

A panel hatch with coded markings.

Bowman had said the dam had no access points on that side.

But there it was.

Clear.

Precise.

Seen only by Daniella's lens.

She swallowed hard.

"What... what is that?"

Mercer's expression sharpened.

"The entrance," he said. "To RIO's original vault. The one even I cannot open without the correct sequence."

Daniella's pulse spiked.

"You can't open it?"

"No," Mercer said calmly. "But you can."

"I don't—"

"Your eye sees patterns instinctively. You captured the sequence unconsciously. Your brain mapped it. You can reconstruct it."

"I didn't SEE anything," she said.

"But you did," Mercer replied. "You've been making the pattern your entire life. You just never recognized it."

She stared at the photo, cold dread creeping up her spine.

"You think I can unlock your vault? That's insane."

Mercer smiled.

"Let me show you something else."

He tapped his tablet again.

Another feed appeared.

Ashling's cell.

She knelt on the floor, trembling.

Her sister—Lina—stood in the opposite glass room, eyes empty, movements unnatural, like a marionette waiting for strings.

"Ashling has been very obedient," Mercer said calmly. "She's given me everything except access to the Behavioral Keys."

Daniella froze.

"What Keys?"

Mercer's eyes glinted.

"Lina has them. They're implanted into her cerebral patterning. She is RIO's memory."

Daniella's breath caught.

"You... you turned her into a computer."

"Not a computer," Mercer corrected. "An asset."

Ashling's scream echoed from the speakers.

"LINA! PLEASE—PLEASE LOOK AT ME—PLEASE—"

But Lina stared straight ahead. Blank. Unfeeling.

Mercer sighed.

"Very tragic. Very predictable. Trauma does create reliability issues."

"You sick bastard," Daniella whispered.

Mercer smirked.

"I've been called worse."

Another scream echoed—this time from Russell.

Stryker kicked him hard in the ribs, forcing him back onto his knees.

"Stop!" Daniella cried out, slamming her hands into the glass so hard it stung. "STOP IT—STOP HURTING HIM!"

Stryker only smiled.

Mercer leaned in. His voice was softer now, almost sympathetic.

"Help me unlock the vault," he said. "And this all ends."

"You expect me to help you after you—"

Mercer cut her off with a dismissive wave.

"You help me, and I will release Russell. I will release Isla. Rivera. Even Bowman. I will let them walk out of here alive."

He paused—but his next words were razor-sharp.

"And Ashling gets her sister back."

Daniella's breath froze.

She looked at the screen—Ashling on her knees, hand against the glass, crying softly as Lina stared past her like a ghost.

Mercer tilted his head.

"They need you, Miss Russo. All of them. You are the only one who can break RIO's last lock."

Tears stung her eyes.

She thought of everything:

Her rooftop photos.

Her lens capturing what others ignored.

Her instincts pulling her into danger without knowing why.

Her entire life—leading here.

"I'm not your weapon," she whispered.

Mercer smiled gently.

"You already are."

Her hand trembled as she reached for the photo on the table.

Not to help him.

But because she saw something he didn't.

Behind the corner reflection—just barely—was a faint outline.

A silhouette.

A woman's.

Ashling's sister.

Alive.

Standing near the vault hatch.

And Lina—

Lina was looking directly at the camera.

At Daniella.

Her blank eyes weren't blank in the image.

They were aware.

And terrified.

Daniella's heart hammered.

She whispered under her breath:

"You asked me to find you."

Russell lifted his head weakly.

"Dani... what are you doing?"

Daniella looked at him, tears spilling silently.

"Saving you," she whispered. "Saving everyone."

She turned the photo.

Looked Mercer dead in the eyes.

"Fine," she said. "I'll unlock your vault."

Mercer's smile widened.

But Daniella's hand slid into her sleeve—

closing around something small, sharp, and metallic.

She'd had it since the tunnels.

Ashling's spare hairpin.

Mercer didn't notice.

Of course he didn't.

He'd never believed she was dangerous.

He wasn't paying attention to her hands—

Only her eyes.

Her greatest weapon.

Daniella stepped toward the white room as the glass door slid open.

Mercer spoke softly.

"Welcome, Miss Russo. Let's finish what we began."

Daniella whispered—

"No."

Let's finish what YOU began.

She stepped inside.

And behind her, the door hissed shut.

CHAPTER 29-YOU HAD ME AT RIO DAM

The white room was colder than the rest of Sector 4.

So bright it felt like stepping into a spotlight.

So sterile it felt like stepping into a lie.

Daniella stood dead center, her pulse racing, her legs trembling from the tranquilizer still bleeding through her system.

Mercer watched from behind the glass, hands folded, eyes hungry.

Stryker stood at the far end, gripping Russell by the back of his shirt, keeping him on his knees like an offering.

Daniella wanted to tear him apart.

But she kept her face calm.

Her breathing controlled.

Her eyes soft, unfocused — the way Mercer expected.

She stepped toward the metal table.

The photograph she'd taken at the dam lay beneath harsh white lights.

Her photograph.

Her curse.

Her calling.

Her power.

Mercer tapped his tablet. "Begin."

Daniella lifted the photo.

And she let herself fall into it.

Not for Mercer.

For Russell.

For Ashling.

For Isla.

For Lina.

For Hale.

For every life Mercer had tried to erase.

She inhaled deeply.

And the world shifted.

She wasn't in the white room anymore.

She was back at Rio Dam.

The wind whipping across the overlook.

The water glittering below.

The camera heavy in her hands.

Russell laughing beside her.

"Don't move," she had whispered then.

She'd felt something shift.

Now she knew what it was.

Her gift didn't come from luck.

It came from pain.

From survival.

From never being seen, so she learned to see everything.

Daniella closed her eyes, letting the memory pulse behind her eyelids.

When she opened them—

Her breath caught.

The photograph had changed.

Not physically— but in her mind's eye, the patterns sharpened.

The reflection grid along the hatch wasn't random metal.

It was a sequence.

A code.

A cipher hidden inside the angles.

Mercer stepped closer to the glass, voice soft. "You see it, don't you?"

Daniella didn't answer.

Her eyes traced the pattern.

Up.

Across.

Down.

Back.

Something triggered in her brain — an instinct she didn't understand, but trusted completely.

Her breath quickened.

Her fingers twitched.

She was mapping it.

Mercer whispered, "Brilliant girl…"

But Daniella wasn't listening.

Because in the reflection— behind the vault hatch, she saw Lina again.

For a split second.

Just a flicker.

Just a flash.

But Lina's eyes weren't blank.

They were full of something fierce.

Something terrified.

Something aware.

Daniella's breath stuttered.

"Lina..." she whispered.

Mercer didn't hear her.

But the hidden camera feed of Ashling's glass cell picked up Daniella's voice—

And Ashling's head snapped up.

ASHLING — Cell 14B

Ashling pressed her hands to the glass.

"Dani...? Dani, what are you doing?"

Her breath fogged the surface.

"Don't help him—don't—"

She slammed her shoulder against the glass. It didn't budge.

She turned toward her sister's chamber.

"Lina... Lina, please look at me. Please—please hear me..."

Lina didn't move.

Didn't blink.

Didn't breathe like a person, but like a machine.

Ashling pressed her forehead to the glass.

"This is my fault..." she whispered. "I left you. I left you to them."

A soft sound made her freeze.

Lina's fingers twitched.

Ashling's heart slammed against her ribs.

"Lina?"

Another twitch—barely there, but real.

Ashling's eyes widened.

"Oh my God. Oh my God—Lina, can you hear me?"

Lina's lips parted—

just a fraction.

And she whispered a single word.

Barely audible.

Barely formed.

But enough to break Ashling's soul.

"...Ash...?"

Ashling dropped to her knees, sobbing.

"I'm here. Baby, I'm here. I'm right here."

Lina blinked.

Her first tear slid down her cheek.

The spell was breaking.

And Mercer didn't know.

RUSSELL — Chamber Hall

Russell tried to lift his head.

His vision swam.

His chest burned.

His limbs felt like stone.

Stryker's boot dug into his back.

"Stay down, lover boy."

Russell snarled. "Go to hell."

"Already been," Stryker said casually. "Didn't like the décor."

Russell spat blood.

But his eyes—

his eyes weren't on Stryker.

They were on Daniella.

She was changing.

He could see it.

Her posture—straight.

Her breathing—controlled.

Her hands—steady.

She wasn't breaking.

She was becoming something else.

Someone unstoppable.

Russell whispered, voice cracking:

"Dani... don't let them win. Don't let them—"

His vision blurred again.

Stryker nudged him with his boot.

"Oh, she'll help us," Stryker said. "She'll give us everything."

Russell gritted his teeth.

"Not her," he whispered.

Stryker smirked. "Oh? And who's going to stop us? You?"

Russell's eyes lifted.

"No," he murmured.

DANIELLA — White Room

Daniella stood in front of the photograph, heart pounding, mind racing.

She traced the reflection grid with her fingertip.

Mercer leaned closer.

"Yes," he whispered. "You're close."

Daniella kept her gaze soft, obedient.

But her words were razor-sharp.

"You know what's funny, Mercer?"

Mercer raised a brow.

"Enlighten me."

Daniella looked up.

Her eyes were steady.

Strong.

Unbroken.

"You think you made me. You think you can use me."

Mercer smiled faintly. "Because I can."

Daniella shook her head.

"No," she whispered. "Because you had me at Rio Dam."

Russell's eyes snapped open.

Stryker froze.

Mercer stilled.

Daniella lifted the photo.

Her voice was a whisper and a roar all at once.

"That was the moment everything changed. Not for you. For me."

She pressed Ashling's hairpin into the seam of the photograph's metal frame.

A tiny pop echoed through the room.

The frame snapped.

And revealed a second layer.

A layer Mercer never knew existed.

His eyes widened.

"No…"

"Yes," Daniella breathed.

Her hands shook—but not with fear.

With fury.

With clarity.

With purpose.

"You think I captured your secrets?" she whispered. "No. I captured hers."

She held the inner layer to the light.

It wasn't a photo.

It was a map.

To Sector 4's true power core.

Not the vault.

Not the hatch.

The failsafe.

A single pressure-point in the foundation that could collapse the entire underground system.

Lina had been standing in front of it.

In her reflection.

Begging someone—anyone—to see.

Daniella saw.

Always had.

Mercer's face contorted.

"NO—"

Daniella turned.

And for the first time in her life— she pointed a weapon with intention.

Not the gun.

Her camera.

She lifted it, pressed her finger to the shutter, and aimed directly at Mercer's image on the glass.

"Smile," she whispered.

Click.

The flash blinded the room.

Stryker stumbled backward.

Russell pushed with his last strength— slamming his shoulder into Stryker's legs.

Stryker fell.

Russell grabbed his gun.

Daniella spun toward the door— just as alarms exploded through Sector 4.

Mercer backed away, shouting orders.

"STOP HER! STOP THEM NOW!"

Daniella's voice cut through the chaos:

"Too late."

Because Daniella Russo—the girl he thought was just a civilian— just became the woman who could destroy RIO from the inside.

And she wasn't done yet.

CHAPTER 30 – THE CLIFFHANGER

Alarms wailed through Sector 4 like the screams of a dying beast.

Red lights pulsed.

Steel shutters slammed into place.

Automated locks clicked in rapid succession.

Mercer shouted orders, but no one could hear him over the chaos he'd built.

Daniella didn't run.

She moved—purposeful, sharp, fluid—driven by adrenaline and the realization that she was no one's pawn anymore.

Russell staggered toward her, blood running down his arm, but still alive, still fighting.

"Dani—" he breathed.

She caught him, her hands on his face, grounding both of them.

"I've got you," she whispered. "I'm not letting you go."

His eyes flickered.

"You shouldn't... You shouldn't have come here."

She pressed her forehead to his.

"Russell, you had me at Rio Dam. I'm not losing you tonight."

His breath hitched—half laugh, half pain.

Behind them—

Stryker rose, rage twisting his face, gun raised.

"Duck!" Russell shouted.

Daniella spun, dragging Russell down as bullets cracked overhead, striking the glass panel behind them.

Ashling's scream cut through the air from her cell:

"DANI—MOVE!"

A blast shattered the glass of her chamber—Rivera had hacked the emergency release—and Ashling barreled out like a storm.

She grabbed Stryker by the back of the head—

—and slammed him into the reinforced wall with a sound that echoed across the chamber.

He crumpled.

But he wasn't dead.

Not yet.

"Where's Lina?" Daniella shouted.

Ashling's breath shook. "Still locked—come on!"

They sprinted toward Lina's chamber.

Daniella's vision blurred—adrenaline and fear burning through her veins.

Bowman and Isla ran toward them—Bowman covered in blood, Isla clutching Hale's letter to her chest like a shield of armor.

"Sector 4 is collapsing!" Bowman shouted. "Mercer triggered the full purge system!"

Daniella stumbled. "Meaning—?"

"Structural failure," Rivera called from the intercom. "The whole thing will fall into the valley. You have less than eight minutes."

Ashling slammed her palm against the glass of Lina's chamber.

"OPEN IT!" she screamed.

Rivera cursed over the comms.

"I'm trying! Mercer's locking me out—"

Mercer's voice echoed through the facility:

"All assets will remain where they are. Do not allow them to escape."

Ashling nearly broke.

"LINA! LOOK AT ME!"

Inside the chamber, Lina blinked.

One slow, painful blink.

"Ash…" she whispered again.

A crack splintered through the glass.

Rivera's voice crackled back:

"I've got it—MOVE!"

The chamber door slid open.

Ashling grabbed her sister, pulling her into her arms, cradling her like the girl she used to braid hair with under the willow tree behind their childhood home.

"I've got you," Ashling whispered. "I'm here. I'm here."

Lina collapsed against her.

She weighed almost nothing.

Her voice was paper-thin.

"Don't leave me again."

Ashling's tears soaked her hair.

"Never. Never again."

Another explosion shook the floor.

Dust rained from the ceiling.

Bowman grabbed Lina's other arm. "We need to MOVE!"

They sprinted toward the exit tunnel—

the one Daniella had mapped in the photograph

the one Lina had tried to show her all along

the one Mercer thought no one else could find.

The facility shook again, bricks tumbling from above.

Smoke filled the corridors.

"Dani!" Russell gasped, stumbling.

His legs buckled—he was going down.

She caught him, gripping his waist with everything she had left.

"I've got you," she said fiercely. "Stay with me."

His eyes fluttered, unfocused.

"Dani... go... I'm slowing you down..."

"You're not slowing me down," she said through tears. "You are the reason I'm moving."

He looked at her—really looked.

"God... I love you."

The world froze.

Then—

A gunshot cracked the air.

Russell jerked in her arms.

Daniella screamed.

Stryker stood behind them, gun smoking, blood running down his temple, eyes wild.

"You should have killed me when you had the chance."

Ashling spun—

rage exploding through her—

She fired three rounds into his chest.

Stryker went down.

This time—

He stayed down.

Bowman grabbed Russell. "He's hit—bad. We need to go!"

Daniella pressed her hand over the wound. Blood poured between her fingers.

"Russell—stay with me—stay—"

His eyes struggled to focus.

"Dani... run..."

"I'm not leaving you."

He smiled weakly.

"You're... stubborn..."

"Russell, don't you dare—don't you dare—"

He lifted a shaking hand.

Touched her cheek.

"Hey... look at me..."

Her tears fell onto his fingers.

"You had me at Rio Dam," he whispered.

Then he went still.

"NO—NO—RUSSELL—"

Her scream tore the air open.

"RUSSELL, PLEASE—PLEASE—"

Bowman grabbed her shoulders.

"Dani—we have to MOVE—"

She clawed at him, wild with grief.

"I'M NOT LEAVING HIM!"

Ashling wrapped both arms around her.

"DANI—LISTEN TO ME! If you stay—if you stay, you DIE—"

The facility buckled violently—

walls collapsing

lights exploding

floors giving way.

Rivera shouted through the comm:

"GET OUT NOW!"

Bowman lifted Russell's unconscious body—

Daniella sobbing, clinging to him—

as they raced into the escape tunnel.

Behind them—

Sector 4 began to collapse

floor by floor

like a sinking mausoleum.

Dust chased them.

Heat singed their backs.

Metal screamed.

Concrete split wide.

Daniella held Russell's hand the entire way.

"Please," she whispered. "Please stay. Please stay."

They burst from the tunnel—into night air, into the roaring wind above the valley— as Sector 4 collapsed into the chasm below.

A deafening crash shook the earth.

The entire facility was gone.

Daniella fell to her knees beside Russell's still body, chest heaving, tears streaking her face.

"Russ... COME ON... PLEASE—"

Bowman knelt beside her, checking his pulse—

A beat.

A second beat.

Slow.

Weak.

But there.

"He's alive," Bowman rasped. "Barely. But alive."

Daniella collapsed over Russell's chest, sobbing with relief.

Ashling held Lina close.

Rivera staggered out of the tunnel coughing.

Isla fell to her knees, clutching her belly, whispering prayers for Hale, for the baby, for all of them.

Silence settled.

Heavy.

Shaking.

Broken.

Then—

the sound of a helicopter echoed across the valley.

Not rescue.

Mercer.

He had escaped.

And he wasn't finished.

Ashling stood, hair whipping in the wind, eyes blazing.

"He's alive," she whispered. "Mercer survived."

Bowman nodded grimly. "He'll come after us."

Rivera wiped blood from her lip. "He'll come after Daniella."

Ashling looked at Daniella—holding Russell, her hands stained with his blood, her heart shattered and blazing all at once.

"Then," Ashling said, voice steel, "we take the fight to him."

Daniella lifted her head.

Her eyes—

once soft—

once untrained—

now burned.

"Finder's Fee," she whispered.

"The price for what he did."

Ashling nodded. "Yes."

Daniella leaned down, kissed Russell's forehead, and whispered:

"Hold on for me. The storm isn't over."

 She stood

Turned toward the valley.

Her silhouette lit by flames.

"This time, we hunt him."

ABOUT THE AUTHOR

Ainsley McHugh writes romantic thrillers that blend love, loss, and the secrets that live between them. Her work explores the fragile line where passion meets danger, unfolding across moody landscapes and emotional tension. Whether she is writing about star-crossed lovers or truths revealed in the dark, her stories are always guided by the quiet certainty that a "happily ever after" is worth fighting for.

A lifelong daydreamer and devoted supporter of the arts, Ainsley draws inspiration from the creativity that surrounds her—music, photography, performance, and the vibrant energy of artistic expression. When she is not crafting worlds of suspense and devotion, she is capturing light through her camera lens, wandering hidden corners of New England, or imagining up new stories by the water with coffee in hand.

Her stories celebrate second chances, vulnerability, and the extraordinary beauty found in ordinary moments— reminding readers that even after the storm, love always has a way of coming home.